With a ha
Dan's arms

Dan backed away. "I didn't mean—" he began.

"It's all right," she rushed to assure him. "I just, I just need to take things slow." Slower than her heart rate, which was belting out a jazz beat against her rib cage. "That okay with you?"

"Look, Jess, I don't want to push it. We're attracted to each other. And that's not a bad thing," Dan said, his grin lightening the mood and putting her at ease. "But if there's something more, we have time to figure it out."

"Good, then." She backed away. Thinking was not an option with six-plus-feet of Dan Hamilton anywhere in the vicinity.

Dear Reader,

Florida has been my home for most of my life. I love the state's natural beauty so much that my house sits in a small clearing surrounded by a tangled acre of pine, scrub oak and palmetto. When I started *The Daddy Catch*, I pictured a heroine who would share both my appreciation for Florida's landscape and my husband's love of fly fishing. Widowed Jess Cofer does exactly that.

She has sworn to turn Phelps Cove into a protected habitat and dreams of the future when her little boy will take his own children fishing there. After years of hard work, Jess's dream is about to come true... until a group of doctors put in a bid for the land.

Thoracic surgeon Dan Hamilton is as determined to build in Phelps Cove as Jess is to protect it. His investment will let him help kids growing up in the foster care system—as he did—and Dan will do whatever it takes to see the project succeed.

But there's more at stake than Phelps Cove when attraction grows between Dan and Jess. There's Jess's little boy, Adam, to consider....

I hope you enjoy *The Daddy Catch*. I love hearing from my readers and invite you to stop by for a visit at www.leighduncan.com.

Leigh Duncan

The Daddy Catch

LEIGH DUNCAN

TORONTO NEW YORK LONDON
AMSTERDAM PARIS SYDNEY HAMBURG
STOCKHOLM ATHENS TOKYO MILAN MADRID
PRAGUE WARSAW BUDAPEST AUCKLAND

Recycling programs
for this product may
not exist in your area.

ISBN-13: 978-0-373-75364-2

THE DADDY CATCH

ABOUT THE AUTHOR

Award-winning author Leigh Duncan spent twenty years moving about the country, but now lives on Central Florida's east coast, not far from where she attended elementary school. Married to the love of her life and mother of two wonderful young adults, she enjoys watching the birds, squirrels and the occasional fox play in her backyard. Leigh loves to write the same kind of books she enjoys reading, ones where home, family and community are key to the happy endings we all deserve.

When she isn't busy working on her next story for the Harlequin American Romance line, she likes nothing better than to curl up in her favorite chair with a cup of hot coffee and a great book. She invites readers to contact her at PO Box 410787, Melbourne, FL 32941, or to visit her online at www.leighduncan.com.

Books by Leigh Duncan

HARLEQUIN AMERICAN ROMANCE
1304—THE OFFICER'S GIRL

For Joe
Your faith and love give flight to my dreams.

Chapter One

"I brought ya some coffee, boss." Sam, On The Fly's manager, placed a sturdy cardboard cup on the edge of Jess Cofer's desk. "You got a few minutes before we open up?"

"Sure." Jess swallowed back a grimace. An employee who wanted to chat before the first customer walked in could only mean her day was rolling further downhill. A shame, because she usually looked forward to Saturday. Most of the time, it meant heading out the door with a fly rod in her hand and a client at her side, but not today. Instead, a last-minute cancellation had forced her to take a hard look at the store's books. She glanced at the tally beneath the expense column and exhaled slowly. Merritt Island's premier fly fishing shop was in trouble.

What would Sam do if he learned the shop's bottom line had taken on water and was headed for the riverbed? Would he quit? Without her most valued employee to run interference with their wealthier, more demanding clientele, she didn't know what she'd do. Bail, probably. She mustered a wary smile for the man in the doorway.

"What's up?" A handful of unruly curls fell across her face. She brushed them aside.

Sam leaned against the doorjamb. He tapped a

rolled-up newspaper against his palm. When he didn't speak, Jess nodded to the paper.

"Any good news in there?" she asked.

The lines around Sam's watery blue eyes deepened. "Prices are up and income is down. Same as usual," he humphed. His voice dropped until Jess could scarcely hear him.

"And old man Phelps died," he murmured. "The paper says he was eighty-six."

Jess slowly settled her red pen on top of her scarred oak desk. The coffee she'd sipped rolled uneasily in her stomach.

"Henry Phelps?"

At Sam's nod, she blinked back a mist of tears and rummaged through the desk drawer for a pack of Kleenex. It lay beneath a hank of ginger bucktail left over from a recent fly tying session. She tugged out a tissue and dabbed her eyes.

"Aw, I shoulda broke the news better." Floorboards creaked as Sam shifted his weight. He shot a hopeful glance toward the display room. "Want me to leave ya alone, boss?"

Jess shook her head. "No, I'll be all right." Henry had been their first client, and after Tom died, it'd been the Florida native's idea to preserve Phelps Cove as a memorial to her late husband. They had worked together on the project until the elderly man's stroke two months ago, but even that hadn't dimmed his dream. They had talked about it when she'd dropped by the hospital last week. Now, Phelps Cove would make a fitting legacy for both Tom and Henry.

The thought settled her stomach, and Jess managed a wobbly smile.

"Henry was a good man. When's the funeral?"

Sam shrugged. "Too early for an obit, but there's a nice write-up on the front page." He unfurled the paper and pointed with a calloused finger. "All about how he made his fortune. Talks a little bit about Phelps Cove and his involvement with Protect Our Environment." He looked down, refusing to meet her eyes. "What's the latest on that?"

The question threatened to send her stomach back into free fall, but Jess caught herself. At 2.5 million dollars for one hundred acres of prime riverfront, not even the state of Florida would be foolish enough to botch the deal. She shook her head, remembering the time a reporter had shoved a microphone at Henry and demanded he explain his motives for selling the land so far below its market value.

"How much money does a body need in one lifetime?" Henry had shot back. "I already got me a fortune. This is my chance at history. Phelps Cove'll be here long after I'm gone."

And now he was. Gone. Jess's shoulders slumped in a world that felt a little emptier.

At a restless sound from the doorway, she straightened. The funding approval was practically a rubber stamp, according to her counterpart in POE, and he should know. The organization was tasked with establishing protected habitats on state-owned land. She aimed a thumb at a poster on the wall behind her.

"Henry always said our great-grandkids should see what Florida looked like before the moon race and theme parks brought in tourism."

"That niece o' his might have different plans," Sam suggested.

She had nearly forgotten about the woman who, according to Henry, rarely ventured out of New York.

"Estelle does prefer life in the big city," she mused. "Henry gave me her number when he flew up for her oldest's graduation. I think it's still in my address book. Let me call her. See where things stand."

When Sam took that as his cue to escape, Jess wished she could go with him. Henry had referred to his niece as "distant" and "self-serving," and Jess was pretty sure she wouldn't like talking to the woman any more than she enjoyed running a business that catered to people who had more money than sense. For the umpteenth time that month, she wondered why she bothered.

Her gaze drifted from the bills and receipts scattered across her desk to her favorite fly rod, propped in the corner of the tiny office. For the first time since she'd arrived at work that morning, she smiled. Tomorrow was Sunday, the one day of the week On The Fly's doors remained closed. A day when she could take her favorite fishing buddy on an excursion to Phelps Cove in honor of two special men, his dad and their old friend. Her smile deepened as she picked up the phone.

A RISING TIDE SALTED THE AIR. Beyond white sand dunes, the surf roared against the shore. Dan Hamilton eyed the bunched shoulders of the figure ahead of him on the coquina walkway and wondered why the other man was so tense. Dan thought he should be the nervous one. This was, after all, his first night of cards with the big dogs of Brevard County's medical society. The occasion prompted a critical self-appraisal and, on the short walk to the converted guesthouse, Dan did just that.

Manners so well rehearsed anyone would think he'd learned them on his mother's knee? *Check*. Bland, Mid-western accent slathered over his native Southern drawl like mayonnaise on a baloney sandwich? *Check*. The same understated labels his peers at the poker table were sure to wear? *Got 'em.*

Satisfied he had ticked off every item with the same careful attention he gave the operating room each time he picked up a scalpel, Dan straightened his shoulders as Bryce Jones III beckoned him into a masculine lair of leather and dark wood. Behind them, the door closed with a swish and a snick, locking out the bright sunshine of a January afternoon on Florida's east coast. Bryce crossed immediately to a bar so well-stocked it deserved its own liquor license. Crystal glasses clinked softly as they settled onto polished wood while Dan fought the urge to wrinkle his nose at the nutty scent of old cigars that drifted in the chilly air.

"Take a look. I think you'll be impressed."

Bryce nodded toward walls peppered with land maps and architectural drawings. On a corner table, beneath spotlights, scale-model buildings and statuary were staggered down a slope to a mock river's edge. A tiny sign read The Aegean.

"You throwing in the towel and moving to Greece?" Dan asked. Not that he believed for a minute the plastic surgeon would walk away from his high-profile client list.

"Me?" Bryce chuckled and poured Scotch without asking Dan's preference. "Nah. You ever been there?"

"No. Not yet." Accepting the glass he was handed, Dan shook his head. He'd barely paid off his school loans and started planning for the future. Ten years of post-grad training among the skilled hands and sharp minds at the University of Florida had put him on the fast track to becoming the best thoracic surgeon in the county, maybe in the state. Once he nailed that recognition, he'd have the clout to achieve his most important goal. After that, there'd be time and money for travel, a hobby. Maybe even a date or two.

Bryce gestured to a painting of Aphrodite, the goddess of beauty.

"You'd love Greece. The islands are peaceful. Private. Exactly the atmosphere my more refined patients expect. Jack and I—you know him, don't you?"

He nodded. Jack Tillman was another plastic surgeon whose family roots ran oak-tree deep. Dan's own were tenacious and hardy, but thanks to the father he'd never met, they were shallow as crabgrass.

Bryce continued. "We want to bring a bit of Greece to our own corner of the universe. There are a thousand cosmetic surgical centers, but ours will offer world-class facilities in tropical seclusion. Deep water access from the Intercoastal Waterway means our patients can recuperate aboard their own yachts." He righted a tiny boat. "Or in one of our cottages. Think of the advantages—no airport hassles, no paparazzi. Just sail south and return looking refreshed and rested after a little touch-up."

At the hint of unexpected possibilities, Dan's chest tightened the way it did on those rare occasions when things in the operating room took an unexpected turn. Thankful his host couldn't see the reaction, he focused on his glass of single malt and took a sip.

"Interesting," he said, leaving Bryce to interpret the remark.

The other man tipped his glass to the arrangement of buildings. "We invited a few friends to invest—Mark, Foreman, Chase. Do you know Chase? He's a thoracic surgeon, like you."

Not exactly like me. Chase spent more time on the golf course than he did in surgery.

"Not well," Dan admitted. In fact, he rarely saw any

of Bryce's circle outside the hospital or fundraisers. To-night's poker party had marked a change in that status, but if he was reading the other doctor correctly, a lot more than cards were on the table.

"They'll all be here tonight." Bryce's focus drifted to the far corner where stacks of chips stood waiting on a green-felted table. "I found the perfect spot on north Merritt Island. It's raw and undeveloped, except for an abandoned orange grove."

Dan followed the man's glance as it slid back to the wall of maps.

"The owner was a miserable old coot." Bryce's eyes narrowed. "He wanted to practically donate the land to the state. Lucky for us, the transfer didn't go through before he died. I tracked down his only heir, who loves the idea of a quick sale. Unfortunately, we've lost an investor." Bryce tsked. "Chase. His ex hired some big-bucks lawyer out of Boca who tied up his last dime until the divorce is final."

Dan squelched the urge to comment on Bryce's callousness. "Bad timing for you," he offered.

"The worst." Amber liquid swirled in Bryce's glass until it sloshed against the sides. "Property like this won't come along again. I'm not going to let it slip past." He knocked back the last of his drink and stared at Dan, his jaw set. "We need someone who shares our goals and interests. Jack mentioned your name."

While the other man spouted facts about leverages and loans and the near certainty of doubling his investment in a year, Dan forced himself to pretend an overwhelming interest in the model architecture. If the profit margin was even half what Bryce said it was, the venture would solidify his financial and professional security.

He wanted in on the deal so bad he could taste the Kalamata olives, but something told him there had to be a catch. "I might be interested," he hedged. "I'd have to take a look at all the details. What's the buy-in?"

"This is the last big parcel without a house or a business in all of Merritt Island. Plus, we'll have to dredge a new channel for the bigger boats."

"How much?" he insisted.

"Half a mil. Maybe a little more. The rest we can finance once the land is ours."

Bryce headed to the bar for another round while Dan did a quick calculation. There was the money he'd set aside to expand his practice. If he scrapped those plans and plundered his retirement funds, he could scrape up half a million dollars. Not overnight, but he could do it.

"Equal shares?"

"Jack and I will take a larger risk for a bigger share of the profits. Even split for the rest."

"What's the time frame?"

"The lawyers have to do their thing, of course." Bryce splashed more Scotch into their glasses. "Some eco group wants the land, but with the niece on our side, we can outbid them. Say, ninety days? Something like that work for you?"

Dan tamped down his enthusiasm with a long pull from the fresh drink. "Maybe," he allowed. "And my role?" A center like The Aegean wouldn't have much call for a thoracic surgeon.

"You'd sit on the board of directors. Lend your name to our advertising campaign. Why don't you take a look at the property?" Bryce held out a folded paper.

Dan slipped the map into the pocket of his leather jacket. He had rounds at the hospital first thing in the morning, but the rest of his Sunday was wide-open. "I'll check it out," he said.

"Fine, then. Let's get together one night next week and crunch some…" Bryce's head tilted at the sound of muffled voices beyond the door. "One last thing," he said quickly. "Before all this happened with Chase, the group of us had planned a fly fishing trip to Belize. It's coming up in April. For obvious reasons, you'd take his place."

"Sounds great," Dan said as the door swung wide enough to let a blast of heat and noise into the darkened room.

Dan hid his astonishment behind a stoic facade while the others, all doctors who'd followed their parents to Harvard and Yale, filed in and drifted to their seats, pulling bills from fat wallets. Even as he exchanged the usual pleasantries with the men, it was hard to grasp the truth. He'd spent his youth so far beyond the wrong side of the tracks, the sound of a passing train was just a whisper in the night. And now, he was a member of the inner circle.

"That's one-fifty to you, Dan," Bryce said.

He wrenched his attention to the present and slid a couple of chips into a growing pot. Over the next week he would visit the property, put his financial guy to work on the money issues and hire an instructor to teach him one end of a fishing rod from the other. But for now, he would focus on the cards he'd been dealt. For the next few hours, he made sure not to win too much and, thinking of the money he needed to raise, made real sure he didn't lose too much.

Chapter Two

The school of redfish was late making its daily foray into the cove.

"Come on, fish," Jess whispered. She eyed a patch of disturbed water that churned toward the spot where her feet were planted in the sandy river bottom. Were those reds? Or worthless bait? Her five-year-old deserved something special. The memory of a spectacular catch. A memory he could pull out whenever the other kids talked about camping or flying model airplanes with their dads.

Jess blinked hard, snugged her sunglasses against her nose and scanned the cove until she caught a flash of coppery fins. The sight loosed a thrill of anticipation, and she took a thick gulp of warm, winter air.

"Hey, Adam," she called quietly. When her only answer was the soft splash of tiny waves dancing beneath a light breeze, Jess ripped her gaze from the fish. Had the boy stumbled into a hole? She'd only taken her eyes off him for a second, but a second was long enough to...

She stifled a laugh as she spotted her son, exactly where she'd last seen him, not six feet from her side.

From his cap with its On The Fly logo to a miniature

pair of waders, Adam looked as if he'd stepped from the pages of the fly fisherman's Dress For Success manual. He even toted a custom-made rod, one she had shortened especially for him. Now, if she could only get him to focus long enough to catch a fish, they'd be all set. But the boy was intent on a nearly translucent jellyfish drifting just beyond his boots. He'd pulled a small net from his pocket and dragged it through the water.

"Mom, is a jellyfish made of jelly? How does he breathe? Where's his nose? Does he have gills like a fish? His legs are all wiggly. Can he walk? How does he get where he wants to go?"

Jess shook her head. And here she thought she'd gotten that degree in marine biology because she wanted to protect the planet's sea life. Who knew it would come in so handy when raising a child?

"Jellyfish can't go wherever they want. The tides and the current push them along. And you're right about noses and gills—they don't have them. They filter oxygen from the water as it passes over them."

"You mean they breathe water? That's gross."

"Not a nice word, Adam." The frown she aimed at her son was wasted while he ran the net through stubby sea grass. "Hey, kiddo. Think you could try to catch a fish or two?"

"Sure, Mom," he answered. He tucked the net into a pocket and tugged enough line from his reel to make a short cast.

When his fly landed with a soft plop not far from where he stood, Jess's teeth worried her lower lip. The boy was a marvel. While most kindergartners could barely tie their own shoes, Adam had been tying flies since he was three. She'd taken him fishing as soon as he could walk across a room without falling. His dad would be proud, she thought, hoping the fish Adam caught today would deepen his ties to the man he'd never known.

She braced herself against a surge of emotions that no longer swamped her the way they had in the weeks and months immediately after Tom's death. She supposed it was true—time did have a way of easing the pain. And five years was a lot of time. She no longer spent hours dwelling on the fight they'd had before he'd headed out that day. Or the clients who'd pressured him to race through a stretch of water known for shifting sand bars.

Not often, anyway.

For Adam's sake, she couldn't be sad—or angry—all the time. A fact she had realized the moment the nurse slipped her newborn son into her arms. Wet and squirming, he had gazed up at her and, when their eyes locked, she'd known. Known that, for his sake, she couldn't wallow in her grief. That it was her job to make the world a better place.

She scanned the cove, satisfied her work along those lines was all but complete. Once the state declared the land a protected habitat, she could rest easy, knowing she'd had a part in saving a little piece of the planet for future generations.

And if creating a lasting tribute to her husband and their friend Henry added to the land's allure, no one could fault her for it. Or think badly of her for hoping Adam caught his first redfish here.

If, that was, the boy caught a fish at all.

It wouldn't be easy. Redfish were elusive. Combine their poor eyesight with a child's limited reach, and the approaching school would need to be right in front of them before Adam had a prayer of twitching his fly beneath a snubbed nose.

"Hey, Adam." She spoke louder this time, wanting to capture his attention for more than a nanosecond. Once she was certain she had it, she dipped her own rod toward the nearby wave and mouthed a silent, "Reds."

When Adam followed her aim, Jess saw two dark eyebrows rise above a tiny pair of polarized sunglasses. She grinned in earnest as his jaw dropped. She'd known grown men to react the same way when they saw their first school of mature reds tearing up the water, the thick golden bodies surging through the shallows, black-spotted tails wiggling in the air as the fish nosed the riverbed for crabs. The sight made her own heart race, and she'd been on the water for most of her life.

"Wow!" Adam's hand blurred as he reeled in the rest of his line.

"Shh." Jess summoned her most patient smile and brought one finger to her lips. "Save the noise till you land one."

The last thing they wanted to do now was to spook the fish. Experience told her it wouldn't take much—a shout, the harsh *kee-uck* of an osprey on the hunt, even a quick movement in shallow water—and every red tail within a hundred yards would disappear. She edged to Adam's side and mimed instructions.

"Slow and easy," she whispered. "Small movements. If you make a noisy cast, they'll get scared."

"I won't, Mom. I can do it." He grinned up at her. "I'm gonna catch me a red."

"I'm going to catch a red," she corrected with an acquiescent shrug. Grammar lessons could wait. The school swam closer.

"Not yet," she coached when Adam's fingers twitched

his line. She understood how badly he wanted to do it. Her own fingers itched to send a fly arcing into the pack. She held back with a stern reminder that the day was all about the boy. One who needed to learn patience.

"Now, Mom? Now?"

"Okay." She signaled when the fish moved within reach. "Pick up your line."

His thin, tanned arms sent a short length into the clear blue. Whipping his rod back and forth, Adam fed a series of loops that would do the trick, even if his form wasn't perfect.

"That's the way," she coached.

From somewhere on the nearby shore, a car door slammed. The noise startled two cormorants from the mangrove trees. They wheeled and turned against the sky, black wings flapping a silent protest. Below them, the school of fish jittered, then stilled.

"Mo-om." Adam's excitement took a nosedive. His fly slapped the water behind him. "What was that?"

Jess could only shrug. "Don't know," she said. "Let's just wait and see what happens."

Hardly daring to breathe, she studied water that had grown so calm it looked oily. She held her breath until the birds returned to their nests. She held it until a half-dozen fins tentatively broke the surface. A few seconds later, a black-spotted tail appeared. When the wary school relaxed enough to continue feeding along the bottom, she exhaled.

"It's okay," she said with more reassurance than she felt. For all their milling about, she counted six or seven tails where before there had been dozens. "The noise rattled them, but give them a minute. They'll calm down. Meantime, get your fly in the air again, and we'll catch you a fish."

On the hill above them, something crashed through the underbrush and a man's voice cut through the air.

"What? Say that again. Reception's lousy out here." If he shouted any louder, they would hear him from the space station. "I'm on north Merritt Island and I need a… What did you say?" More bushes rattled and a branch snapped. "Hello? Hello? Son of a gun."

"Hey, mister. Be quiet up there." Adam raised a booted foot.

"Adam, don't move," Jess protested.

Her warning came too late. The boy had already stomped the riverbed. Before circles spread out from his legs, fish shot out of the cove in a volley of torpedolike ridges.

"Look!" Adam cried. "They're getting away."

He loosed line over the flat, empty water they left behind. His fly sank into a clump of river grass. He gave a sharp tug or two. The water barely rippled. Nothing bit. He turned a stormy face toward Jess.

"Where'd they go? Why'd they leave like that?"

Behind the safety of her sunglasses, Jess blinked tears of disappointment. She wanted Adam to catch his first red in the cove even more than he did. But there were lessons to be learned, and her son might as well learn them now. She cleared her throat and hooked a thumb over her shoulder at the shore.

"Noise," she explained. She pointed to Adam's foot. "And movement. They got scared and they bolted. Reds do that sometimes."

Adam's mouth trembled. "Those were my fish. I was gonna catch a big one. We hafta go after them." He started toward the deeper water.

Jess lunged for the hem of his shirt and held on.

"Tell you what," she offered. "I have to work the

next couple of days, but we'll come again. Soon. And next time, we'll bring the boat. That way, if the school spooks, we can go after them."

Adam's face darkened. His voice rose. "Let me go. Those are my fish. I want to catch a fish."

"We can't, Adam. It's too deep. Plus, there are dredge holes. Remember me telling you about them?" Back in the '20s, dredging efforts had deepened the river channels. Birds now nested on the spoil islands created by piles of sediment, and fish hid wherever equipment had left pockets in the river bottom. The thought of her only child falling into one was the stuff nightmares were made of.

Adam dropped his rod and reel into the river and crossed his arms. "I don't wanna fish anymore. I wanna go home."

Jess sighed. Her son might be a fly fisher, but he was still just five years old.

"Adam," she said. "That's not the way you treat your equipment. Pick up your rod."

"Make *him* do it. He's the one who scared the fish." Adam aimed an accusatory finger toward the bluff that ran along the shoreline.

From a thicket of pepper trees and palmettos came the sound of crackling branches. Jess caught a glimpse of white through the final layer of brush before a tall man emerged onto the narrow shore. She scrutinized the stranger, who wore clothes more suited to the office than wandering around the wilderness. He pulled leaves and twigs from his thick, dark hair.

"Hey," he called with a wave and an innocent-looking grin. "How's the fishing?"

Jess flexed the fingers of her free hand. It hadn't taken the vultures long to hear of Henry's death and swoop in, looking for easy pickings. This one had "land developer" written all over him. Well, she had news for him. He might as well keep right on walking.

"Fine." She gave him her best dirty look. "Until you showed up."

While Adam drummed a steady, "I want to go home. Come on, let's go. Can't we just go home," the newcomer moved to the river's edge.

"Everything all right?" he called.

"Not really," Jess mumbled. Some days the fish bit. This time, the day did.

Twenty yards of water drowned their voices. The stranger cupped a hand to one ear and shouted, "What'd you say?"

For the moment, Jess ignored him in favor of her son.

"Adam," she said. "Listen to me. We'll leave in a few minutes."

Her promise didn't slow her son's litany of complaints any more than it wiped the signs of an impending melt-down from his face. She took a deep breath. Bribery was not her favorite trick in the motherhood bag, but if Adam didn't stop carrying on, she'd never be able to convince the stranger he had come to the wrong place.

She bent down until she and her son were nose-to-nose.

"If you'll let me talk to this man for two minutes we'll stop for nuggets 'n' fries on the way home." Nuggets were his favorite, and the way business had tanked at On The Fly lately, fast food had become a luxury.

"I wa— Really, mom?"

"Yes, but you have to stand right here beside me until I say we can go."

"Yes, ma'am. I will."

Jess gave her son the I-mean-business-mister look and bit back a grin when he turned into a statue. Her voice rose. "All that noise you made cost my son the red he was going to catch," she said pointedly.

"The red?" The man on the shore didn't seem to understand.

"The fish my son was about to catch," she explained.

"Hey, sorry," he called. He had the good grace to look abashed. "Anything I can do?"

"I think you've done enough, thank you." Jess tucked a few errant strands of hair beneath her hat. "If you'll just go back the way you came, we'll call it even."

OKAY, HE PROBABLY DESERVED THAT. He hadn't tried to be quiet while slipping and sliding down the hill or working his way through the brush along the shore. But how was he supposed to know fish were so sensitive?

Dan eyed the fifty or sixty feet of lapping river between the fly fisher and himself. No matter how he pitched his voice, he'd either have to shout to make himself heard or move closer. He glanced down. Going barefoot wasn't an option, not with horseshoe crabs and who-knew-what-else hugging the bottom of the river. The Ferragamos he'd worn on early-morning rounds were now, thanks to an unplanned trek through the jungle, scuffed and gouged beyond repair. Sandspurs had snagged his pants. Beggar-lice clung to the fine wool. A little water couldn't make the damage any worse.

"Sorry," he repeated. He waded into the rippling current until it reached midcalf. "I didn't mean to cause a problem."

Not that he wouldn't have taken a closer look at the intriguing pair he'd spotted from the bluff. The kid made fly fishing look easy while the woman's gestures were so fluid she reminded him of a dancer. He hadn't wanted to interrupt them, but they were the only other people around, and he needed help.

Now that he was closer, he could see it had been worth the trouble.

Though sunglasses and a floppy hat hid the woman's face, he followed the trail of her slender neck down to a tan shirt and a fishing vest that hinted at plenty of curves. Below a narrow waist, khaki brushed against her smooth thighs. Thankful he had his own sunglasses to hide behind, he looked on in admiration as she tugged her hat from her head and shook heavy blond curls onto her shoulders.

Dan started and sucked in a breath. When had she turned to face him?

"This," she pointed to the land behind him, "is private property. What gives you the right to be here?"

He rubbed the back of his neck where the sun warmed it. The woman couldn't have any idea how temper made her face glow. If she did, she'd keep that look under wraps. As it was, he had trouble taking his eyes off her, much less coming up with an answer that kept plans for The Aegean a secret without leaving him stranded in the middle of nowhere.

"I could ask you the same question," he said, hoping to turn the tables.

"*I* was invited," she answered. She cocked a slim hip and propped one hand on it. "I run a guide service, and the owner lets—let me bring clients fishing out here."

The woman's attitude practically demanded he goad her a little. "And he's your client?" Dan nodded to the kid.

"A little mother-son bonding time," she answered quickly.

An unfamiliar feeling tightened Dan's throat when her free hand dropped protectively onto the child's shoulder. He rubbed his chest, pushing aside faded memories.

"Too bad the big one got away. Thanks to you." She squared her shoulders. "And you never answered my question. Why are you here?"

He didn't see any point in telling an outright lie. "I heard this property might be for sale. You say you know the owner. Think it's true?"

"Sh—" With a look at her son, the woman cut off whatever she'd intended to say. She kicked her foot against the riverbed, sending up a spray of water. "I don't know where you got your information, but you couldn't be more wrong. The state wants the land for a protected habitat."

According to talk around the poker table Saturday night, The Aegean group was mere weeks away from changing the lock on the gate. But now wasn't the time to share that bit of news.

"Looks like I wasted a trip, then," he said.

"Looks like. Maybe you'd better head back now. Before the sun gets to you."

"I would, but my car is mired in a sandpit up there." Dan pointed toward the bluff.

The minute he'd stepped out of the sturdy BMW and seen only the top half of his rims peeking over the dirt, he'd known he was in serious trouble. As impossible as it had looked, he'd tried to free the vehicle. He pushed. He rocked. He kicked the tires. The car hadn't budged. At that point, any sane person would have asked for a little help.

Any normal person would give it.

Since the fly fisher continued to stare at him without offering assistance, she had to be something else. He searched for a compromise while she stole some of the sunshine from the day by stuffing her hair back under her soft-sided hat.

He tugged his cell phone from a back pocket. "Thought I'd call a tow, but—" he waved the device "—no service."

She swept a hand through the air. "No cell towers," she corrected. "No coverage at this end of Merritt Island."

Dan made a mental note. The Aegean group would need to rectify that little problem before the first bull-dozer descended.

"Think I can hitch a ride?" he asked. At the gate, sunlight glinting off spiderwebs in broken sections of chain link had seemed a good indication that no one but the investment group was interested in the property. Now, with a hundred acres of wilderness behind him and two miles of river out front, the isolation wasn't nearly so comforting.

The woman pointed down. "My truck's on the other side of the cove and the river bottom's full of oyster shells. Without boots, you'd cut your feet to ribbons. Or step on a stingray. But there's a radio in my truck. If you can hang out for a couple of hours, I'll send a tow. You have water?"

There was plenty in the car. "I'm good, thanks."

Seconds later, the boy took off. As he pounded through shallow water toward the far shore, the woman turned. "Duty calls," she said over one shoulder. "Can't let him out of my sight. The way my day is going..."

If she finished the sentence, Dan didn't catch it before she hurried after her child. The effort flexed the muscles of her trim calves. He tried without much success to quit staring after her. If the blonde happened to turn around and catch him, he was pretty sure she wouldn't like it much.

Dan shook his head. What was he thinking? For all he knew there was a Mr. Fishing Guide somewhere. And a kid—even a cute one—only complicated matters.

Not that he was looking for a date. Or even interested.

No, all he needed was a tow, and it was enough that she'd agreed to send one. With that in mind, Dan plunged back the way he'd come, determined to wait by his car for the truck's arrival.

Ten minutes and a moderately steep climb put him at the top of the bluff where he wiped a light film of sweat from his forehead. Below, nothing more interesting than a stork moved along the water's edge. Through dense thickets of palmetto ahead, he spied several gnarled citrus trees, the unpicked fruit shriveled down to small, brown balls. Vine and brush grew everywhere else. With no hundred-year-old oaks to give the environmentalists heartburn, the site made the perfect location for Bryce's private clinic, and he wondered why no one had already snapped it up.

They should have.

So many houses crowded the swath of land between Cocoa and Cocoa Beach, he'd never have guessed this much undeveloped acreage existed. To the north, the building where space launch vehicles were prepped for takeoff towered above the treetops. Another plus. With Kennedy Space Center so close, the clinic could advertise front row seats to rocket launches, something their über-rich target market would appreciate.

Air whistled, low and tuneless past his lips.

He'd give it another two hours before he struck out
on foot. Any longer, and he risked getting stuck in the
woods after dark. Million-dollar views or not, he didn't
relish the thought of a night in the wilderness without
food, water or insect repellant.

Or snake boots, he added, when something long and
black slithered past. He waited until the snake disappeared into the brush before he stepped onto the narrow
dirt track that led back to his car.

Chapter Three

That evening, after baths and prayers, kisses and hugs and bedtime routines guaranteed to keep the monsters at bay, Jess slid onto a kitchen stool. The stranger from the cove fresh in her mind, she paged through her address book until she found the number Henry had given her. Moments later, a phone rang twice before someone in Manhattan answered.

"Estelle," she began after introducing herself. "I was so sorry to hear about your uncle's passing. Henry spoke quite highly of you. If there's anything I can to do help now that he's gone..."

Though her tone suggested otherwise, Estelle Phelps said she appreciated the call. "Uncle Henry will be buried in the family plot, but his instructions included a local service. I've asked one of your mortuaries to handle the arrangements."

"Any idea when...?"

"Next month sometime. With all the details of his estate to sort out, I'm afraid I couldn't possibly make it down before then."

The indifferent attitude combined with the clipped words, so different from Henry's warm drawl, made Jess lift her eyebrows.

"I'm sure you have a million details to sort out, so I won't keep you. But maybe we could get together while you're here?"

"Oh?" Mild surprise filled Estelle's voice. "Did you know my uncle well?"

Though her pulse began to race, Jess moved to the other purpose of her call. "I helped Henry with his Phelps Cove endeavors. The preserve will make a lasting memorial to him." And to Tom, she added silently.

"According to my lawyers, that sale isn't final yet."

"Not officially," Jess admitted. The muscles at the back of her neck tightened. Not even forty-eight hours had passed, and Henry's niece had already spoken with her lawyers? The thought triggered a wave of concern that sent her to the roll-top desk she used as a home office. Juggling the phone under her chin, she wiped a light coating of dust from the binder that held her POE notes and flipped through until she found the agenda for the state legislature.

"All the arrangements are in place," she said firmly.

The voice on the other end of the line sharpened. "The state's offer is far below what I can get elsewhere, Ms. Cofer. You might as well know I intend to fight this ridiculous sale."

Jess squeezed the phone in a tight grip. "Your uncle signed contracts. Once the funding is approved during the current legislative session, it's a done deal." Of that she was certain. Her backside still bore calluses from all the hours she'd spent sitting in attorneys' offices while Henry and his lawyers iron-cladded the agreement.

"Ms. Cofer, if the money is released on schedule, I'll be forced to honor Uncle Henry's wishes. But if circumstances change…" Estelle's voice trailed into a guarded laugh.

We'll lose the land.

"I'll make sure they don't." Jess crossed her fingers. Senators and representatives would meet in Tallahassee well into spring, giving her plenty of time to convince Henry's heir to hop onboard POE's bandwagon. "Let me take you to lunch when you're here, and we'll talk about it."

Estelle sighed. "I suppose I could fit you in. We'd have to meet after the memorial. I'll have my secretary work out the details with you. Ciao."

Jess grimaced and hung up. "Aw, Henry," she murmured. "If you'd known how much dying would complicate things, I bet you'd have hung on another three months."

Maybe she should have kept the stranger in the cove talking this afternoon. Should have found out all she could about him and his plans. Certainly, there was more to learn besides the fact that he was tall, dark and handsome….

The notebook spread open on her desk beckoned and she shook that last thought aside. Leafing through hundreds of pages every time someone raised a question wasn't good enough. Not even close. She padded into the kitchen and, knowing it was going to be a long night, put a fresh pot of coffee on to brew. With Henry gone, it was up to her to see their dream become reality. She wouldn't let either of them down.

Chapter Four

A shadow passed across Dan's office desk. The movement broke his concentration on a journal article touting advances in thoracic medicine. He looked up in time to glimpse a pelican soaring over the Indian River. A fishtail drooped, wet and glistening, from its pouched beak. Another bird swooped in to steal the prey, and the two flew through aerial maneuvers that would make World War II dogfighters jealous.

He stilled, leaving Watson, Rice and Blake's "Lost Indian" to play on minus his tapping foot. The battle reminded him of the way the fishing guide had taken him to task. He stared at the now empty sky thinking it was too bad they'd squared off against each other. He was in need of an instructor, and he could easily picture himself heading down the river in a fast boat, the comely fly fisher at his side.

Someone in the outer office laughed. The noise drifting through his closed door was a reminder not to waste time daydreaming about a woman who was wrong for him. Even if she did happen to be available—for fishing, he reminded himself sternly—the way she'd bristled at his interest in Phelps Cove pitted her against all he wanted to accomplish. His phone rang and he straightened at the unusual interruption of his lunch hour. He reached for the receiver.

"Dan Hamilton, here," he said with a nonchalance long-perfected to soothe anxious patients.

"Dan, it's Glen. You got a minute?"

He always had time for the man who had taken him in and kept him on the straight and narrow. "What's up?" he asked. He marked his place with a slip of paper and slid the journal aside.

"It's Sean Hays," Glen said. "He's dead set on dropping out of school. If you're free, can you meet us in the lobby?"

Already on his feet, Dan asked, "He's with you?" Despite a rough start, Sean was a straight-A student. If the boy wanted to quit now, only months before graduation, the reason had to be serious.

"In the car. I've been trying to talk some sense into him all day. I've gotten nowhere. Maybe you'll have better luck."

"Crap," Dan muttered. Glen was pretty good at getting kids to open up, and they both knew it. "I'll be right down."

A quick exchange of words, and Glen elected to stay behind while Dan made his way through the lobby doors. In the parking lot, he shook the hand of a man-boy who towered over his own six-feet-two-inches. Basketball had been created for people like Sean and, if the loose-limbed senior stuck to the program, he'd make the starting string at Dan's alma mater.

"Let's walk," he said and headed for the retaining wall that ran along the river. "You got this all worked out? How're you going to support yourself?" There wasn't time to shoot the bull with the kid. If he couldn't change Sean's mind, there were immediate steps to take.

Like finding a place for the boy to live. Glen and his wife, Maddy, put up with a lot of shenanigans, but no one broke the stay-in-school rule and remained under their roof.

"I'll get an apartment." Sean's soft voice belied an aggressive nature that served him well on the court. "I got a good job at Home Depot. I'm working thirty hours a week, and in a year, I'll make floor manager. It's enough."

Not by a long shot. Without a high school diploma, the hardware chain was unlikely to move him forward. Even if it did, a year without insurance or benefits meant the kid's life teetered on the edge of disaster.

"Man, we had a plan," Dan said. The state provided free tuition for the handful of foster kids who stayed in school long enough to use it. Sean's grades had earned scholarship money for the rest. "You're going to stay with Glen till the summer session starts at UF. Once you're there, your coaches, they'll watch out for you. You'll play some ball, get a good education, and build a life—a real life—for yourself."

Sean folded massive hands across his chest. "Like I told Mr. Glen, I gotta do this."

Pressing the issue wasn't going to change the boy's mind. Dan tried another angle.

"Okay, so you have to. Eight bucks an hour won't put much food on the table. You'll still have rent to pay. What's your backup plan?"

Sean's chin rose. "I'm big and I'm strong. I can pick up another job if I have to."

"You're also smart." Too smart to throw away his future over a dead-end job. There had to be more at stake. "What's all this about, Sean? I thought we had you squared away."

"It's time for me to step up and be the man of my family." Sean's bluster faded, and his shoulders rounded in a way that spoke volumes. His hands dropped to his sides. "It's my sister, Doc."

"Regina?"

The boy nodded. "I need to take care of her."

Dan winced at the naiveté of kids who thought they could make it on their own. Much less, care for someone else.

"We've been over this," he said. "Eighteen's too young to be fending for yourself, but the state won't cover you anymore." His own anger at a system that cut kids loose while most were still in high school threatened to filter through. He took a breath before he continued. "The best thing is to get your own education. Then, you can turn around and help her."

"Be too late then. They're movin' her into a group home. She's too little for that shit." Sean's voice strained and tapered into silence.

Dan's steps slowed. The boy's half sibling hadn't inherited his genes for size or strength. She'd have a tough time holding her own in the winner-take-all atmosphere of a facility that was more institution than house. Knowing the only constant about foster care was that no one stayed in one place very long, he still had to ask, "What happened? We had it worked out for her to live with the Mayers."

Sean's tone turned derisive. "He got laid off and lost the house. They're movin' at the end of the week."

Dan suppressed a groan. The family had taken in six kids. Family Services would be hard pressed to place all of them. Despite her size, Regina was the oldest and a prime candidate for the housing option of last resort.

"I promised my mom I'd watch out for her. Now I need to make good." Sean's voice wavered.

His good intentions wouldn't protect his sister when they both got tossed out on the street, but the boy would never agree that she was better off *in* the system than *out* of it.

"Let me make some calls, okay?" Dan ran down a too-short list of alternatives and knew better than to make promises. He wrapped one arm around the kid and pulled him close enough to give him a bear hug which, considering Sean outweighed him by fifty pounds, was a pretty good analogy. "You go on to school with Mr. Glen and give me a chance to work this out. I'll do my best."

Having spent three-quarters of his life being shuffled from one temporary home to another, Sean knew the score. His chin jutted out. "It might take more than that." His voice firm, he stepped back. "You got till the end of the week when the Mayers move out. After that, I don't have a choice."

All long legs and arms, the boy loped across the parking lot. The Jeep he folded himself into bore scars from hordes of young men who had taken their first driving lesson behind a steering wheel that was practically held together by duct tape and prayer. Dan had been one of those boys, and he wanted to tell Sean that life wouldn't always be this hard.

"Stick with the program," he whispered.

When he was a kid, Glen and Maddy had helped him make the right choices, but they couldn't do it all. One day, Connections House would be the answer. For the past few years, Dan had been planning the home for kids who'd "aged out" of the foster system. But he still needed a lot more revenue to get started. Profits from The Aegean would finally allow him to make his dream a reality. Once the house was up and running, a kid like Sean would have a place to live and people to help him stay in school, teach him how to shop, keep a job, open a checking account. It wouldn't solve all that was wrong with the system, but it was a start.

Wishing he could open the house today, Dan trailed a group of office workers heading back from lunch. He gave Glen's shoulder a gentle squeeze, waking the man from the nap he'd managed in one of the dozen chairs scattered throughout the busy lobby.

"It's Regina," Dan announced. "He's convinced he has to take care of her. He'll drop out if he has to. Did you know the Mayers were moving?"

"Well, that's not good." With a sigh that said he'd been down this road more often than he liked, Glen rose and stretched. "You gotta admire the boy's sense of responsibility, though."

The lines around Glen's face had deepened and his hair had turned from salt-and-pepper to silver in the years since Dan'd moved out on his own. His foster parents no longer took in young children, and he squelched the idea of asking them to make an exception.

"Yeah, but you and I both know it won't last. Oh, they'd be fine for a while. We could get 'em into subsidized housing. Sean's got a lot of heart so they'd make it work...till one of them got sick. Or until there were cutbacks at the store and he was laid off. Then, they'd wind up on the street, or worse, and we'd lose two lives rather than one."

"That's what I love about you." Glen nudged him with an elbow. "Always looking on the bright side."

"I'll make some calls, find her a new placement."

"Look at it this way—at least it's something we can

fix. If he'd gotten some gal pregnant… Well, that'd be another story."

Dan laughed, but there wasn't anything funny about teenage pregnancy. He was living proof they didn't always turn out like those sappy movies of the week on the cable channel, though his mom had done the best she could.

"I've got some news you'll want to hear," he said. "Remember me telling you about Bryce Jones? Plastic surgeon, head of the Medical Society. I played poker with him and some guys the other night."

"Oh, yeah?" Glen prodded. "How much did you take them for?"

"You know me too well, but this time I broke even. Had to." He let his smile broaden. "You're talking to the newest member on The Aegean's board of directors. It's an elite cosmetic surgical center, and I've been asked to join."

"You're not moving to plastic surgery, are you?"

"Of course not," he answered. "But with the money I make from this, I can fund Connections House, and then some. I've been out to look at the land. It's a great site. Right on the river."

"You mean expensive." Glen's unibrow furrowed. "You have enough to buy your way in?"

"If I make some adjustments," he said without going into the details.

He eyed the man who stood with his arms crossed and a scowl on his face. Glen had never been satisfied with simple answers. "You know Bryce's people are the real movers and shakers around here. Acceptance into their crowd means more referrals, more involvement with the community. It means security." He rocked back on his heels. "Both for myself and the practice." Wasn't that why he pushed himself? And not just for him or Connections House. One day, he'd find the right woman and they'd have children. He wanted to give them all the security, love and acceptance he'd never had.

Glen's look turned speculative. "So how come you're not out having lunch with the boys today?"

Dan shook his head. "Be thankful you called when you did. You might have missed me." Not that he would have met Bryce and company, even if they'd asked. Lunch hours were reserved for phone calls, chart work and the latest medical journal. "Going to do a little fly fishing, though."

"Fishing?" Glen snorted. "Too smelly. Too many barbs. How'd you get into that?"

"Taking a jaunt down to Belize with the guys this April."

Glen's chuckles echoed across the marble floor. "You? Going after sailfish? This I gotta see. You have room for one more?"

Dan tilted his head to give the older man a sideways look. The quarry he'd imagined were much smaller than monstrous fish with swordlike snouts. "What makes you think—"

"What else would it be? Belize is famous for 'em."

"Don't worry," Dan said as much for his own benefit as Glen's. "I'll be ready by the end of March."

"Yeah? Good luck with that," Glen chortled before turning serious. "I worry about you. If this fishing thing doesn't work out, you need to find another hobby. All work and no play makes for an unbalanced life."

Glen's sermons on what to do with nonexistent free time were all too familiar. "I run. I work out," Dan protested.

"So do I, but only because it's good for me. You need to have some fun, my boy."

"I'll work on that," he said drily.

"See? That's what I mean," Glen shot back. "With you, it's all work."

"Okay, okay," he conceded with a wry smile. His pager saved him from defending himself further by emitting a soft chirp. "Sorry, Glen," he said, "I have to go. Appointments are backing up. My office manager's getting antsy."

"You'll take care of finding a better place for Regina, then?"

"No problem." Dan scuffed a foot against the floor. "Well, there's always a problem. But I'll manage. Now though, I have to run."

Since Mondays were largely devoted to postsurgical consults, the progress of his patients made for a busy, but rewarding, afternoon. Though Dan frowned over a slowly closing incision and scheduled an extra follow-up later in the week, he was pleased to see that even his brittle diabetic was on the mend. The results added the tiniest boost to his confidence, which helped ease the fears of two new surgical candidates as he walked them through what they should and should not expect from their operations.

By five, when the last patient headed down the hall, he returned to his desk where making good on his word to Sean once again took top priority. Although there was little chance she'd have the answer he wanted, his first call went to Sarah Magarity, Regina's social worker. The young redhead juggled so many foster kids and all their many problems that he had her cell number on speed dial.

"If you're not calling to tell me you've gotten married

and want to adopt a couple of kids, you're wastin' my time, Dan."

He smiled at the tireless woman's spunk. "Yeah, I love you, too, Sarah. How are you doing with placing the Mayer kids? Six, aren't there?"

"I found homes for three. The Smith girl's mom moved back in with her parents, so she'll take the littlest one. That leaves two, and I don't have any choice but to put them in Group."

"Two?" Dan didn't try to mask his surprise. "I thought it was only Regina. How old's the other one?"

Sarah's pause prepared him for bad news. "Twelve," she said at last.

Hard at any age, the regimented atmosphere of a group home was especially tough on preteens. He should know. He'd spent a mercifully short time in one just after his mom died. Although he'd been thirteen, it had been a very unpleasant experience and he'd noticed how much worse it was on the younger ones. "And there's nobody else? You're sure?"

"People have a hard enough time putting food on their tables. No one's looking for another mouth to feed." The few who thought of foster care as an easy way to make money, didn't stay in the program long. The monthly stipend barely covered essentials.

Sarah ran down her list of go-to people, the ones she usually counted on to squeeze in another child or two. There were no vacancies until she reached the particularly kindhearted Carol Shea.

"She's out. After that last fiasco with the Johnson kid, she said she couldn't take it anymore. Shame, too. She was one of our best."

Dan understood. Carol had been burned one too many times. Most foster parents kept their emotional distance.

The ones who didn't were better for the kids, but sometimes paid a heavy price when biological parents swept in and ripped their children out of a perfectly good situation for one far worse. But history wasn't likely to repeat itself with Regina. Her mom was in Lowell, serving twenty-to-life with no chance of parole.

"Let me see if I can make something work," he said, mapping out the best approach. He jotted down the woman's phone number and street address. "I'll swing by. I'm harder to say no to in person," he said with a grin.

Two hours and a whole lot of sweet-talking later, the grandmotherly Carol Shea had agreed to take in the two young girls for a month. After that, well, they'd just have to see how things went. The solution wasn't perfect, but in the chaotic world of foster care, Dan knew it was as good as he was likely to get.

Chapter Five

Jess shored up the corners of a fake smile as she escorted her top candidate for The Worst Customer list to the door of On The Fly.

"Let me know what you decide about that ten-weight," she said, her way of reminding the frequent visitor that he'd asked her to put the expensive rod on hold.

"Sure, Jess. Sure. How 'bout I let you know over drinks Saturday night? We could go to Port Canaveral, watch the cruise ships dock for the weekend."

Jess shook her head. Mr. Not So Charming needed some new material. He'd made the same play on his last visit to the shop. "Sorry, Bill," she said. "No can do."

Weekend clients from out of state meant she'd be up at four, at the boat ramp by six, and doling out coffee and donuts on her way to her favorite fishing spot before the sun cleared the horizon. By the time nightfall rolled around and all her gear was prepped and ready for the next day, she'd be too tired to hold her head up, much less play the flirt, even if she wanted to. Which she did not.

"Let me know if you change your mind," Bill insisted. "You've got my number."

She had his number, all right. Once the door swung

closed behind him, she clutched the handle as much to prevent the man from coming back as for support. She stood guard until he tossed his purchases—a too-small bag of hand-tied flies—into the back of his SUV and eased the car onto Grove Street from the parking lot at the edge of Merritt Island's bustling business district. Only then did she let her fake smile fade.

"How did I let myself get talked into this? What was I thinking?"

She'd never wanted the hassles of running a store. Of juggling schedules for ten employees or making sure the parking lot was freshly paved. On The Fly had been Tom's dream, not hers. He had taken her idea of a fishing guide service and turned it into the area's best fly fishing shop. He'd made it seem so easy, glad-handing the demanding customers until they walked out the door carrying twice what they'd come in to buy. He never even flinched at their outlandish requests. If someone wanted a rod in a particular color, he built it. If they wanted green bullet shrimp instead of the standard copper and brown, he tied them.

Yeah, and if they wanted to fly across treacherous water, he did that, too.

He'd always taken the dare, enjoyed the risk. Only this time, he'd paid the cost. Leaving her to manage their business. Alone. To raise their child. Alone. To bear the full weight of responsibility. Alone.

She leaned forward and knocked her head against the hardwood door frame.

"Problems, Jess?" came a familiar voice.

"Nothing that rolling back the clock a few years wouldn't cure," she whispered.

She left off butting her head and crossed to the register where Sam counted the day's miniscule take. She hooked a thumb over her shoulder at the nearly empty parking lot.

"I spent two hours showing Bill every rod in stock, and all he bought was twenty-five dollars worth of flies. That's it for me. Next time Prince Charming shows up, you handle him."

Sam shook his head. "I don't think he comes here to see me."

"Really. Ya think?"

From the sales counter, Sam tsked. "Sarcasm, Jess. Not your most endearing quality."

"He asked me out again." She twirled one finger in her hair.

"Okay, so he's not your type." The manager studied the floor. "It's time you got a social life, though. Maybe not with him, but with somebody."

She felt her eyes widen. Since Tom's death, Sam had assumed the role of a Dutch uncle, offering his opinion on everything from the rods they stocked to the guide service she hoped would take up the slack in On The Fly's sagging bottom line. Though she counted on his frank advice, her social life had remained off-limits. Until now.

"Dating so does not enter into my immediate plans," she answered. "Between the shop and Adam, I can hardly catch my breath. And now that Henry's gone, things with Phelps Cove are a mess, too."

"I'm just saying you should think about it, is all," Sam persisted.

"Okay, Sam, have it your way." She had no idea what had prompted his sudden interest in her love life, but she wasn't going to let it slide. "I'll play along. Let me take some notes." She pressed an imaginary pen to an imaginary pad. "Let's see. I need someone who has a job. And enough money to be comfortable, but not so much it turns him into an arrogant and demanding jerk. I know, how 'bout Li'l Al? At least then I wouldn't have to cook, because he still lives with his *mother*."

She paused to take a breath and shook her head. The mechanic hadn't said a word about the man he'd towed out of Phelps Cove.`

"Jeez, Jess. I'm not saying you should marry the guy. Just go to dinner. Catch a movie. Get—" Sam's ears turned as red as a Clauser minnow "—you know."

"Sam, I cannot believe you," she sputtered. More slowly, she added, "I am not looking for a bed partner. If I were, it wouldn't be on a casual date. And I do have my own criteria. Anyone I date has to like kids—specifically mine. And he has to enjoy fishing—specifically fly fishing. And it wouldn't hurt if he was easy on the eyes."

"I don't know, Jess. Maybe this wasn't such a good idea after all." Sam slammed the drawer of the cash register closed.

For a second there, she'd almost hoped they'd come up with a likely candidate. "Maybe someday." She softened. Maybe after the state bought Phelps Cove and POE turned it into a protected habitat. After On The Fly was a tad more solvent. Years from now, when Adam was much, much older.

"So, what about him?" Sam asked as the bell over the shop's door tinkled.

Jess blinked, momentarily speechless. There, walking through the door and into her store, was the man from the river. Half convinced she had conjured him from thin air, she closed her eyes, counted to ten and took another look.

Well, he was easy on the eyes. With broad shoulders,

a trim waist and long, lean legs, he had a body that would entice any woman to cast a line in his direction.

She twisted a curl around one finger and told herself she wasn't interested. The perfectly good pair of leather shoes he had dunked in salt water showed a sense of entitlement so ingrained it made her blood boil. Granted, his looks could generate a whole different kind of heat. But since he hadn't known enough to wear a hat over all that dark, wavy hair, she knew he was not the outdoors type.

And so, not her type. Not at all.

"Sam," she hissed, turning to face her manager. "That's the guy who's interested in buying Phelps Cove. What the spit is he doing here?"

"I don't know," Sam answered, "but he's on his way over."

"You handle him," she said, overruling Sam's grumbles. "I'll be upstairs in the apartment."

SMOOTHED AND POLISHED BY COUNTLESS hands, the brass-belted tree limb that served as On The Fly's door handle was whimsical enough to put an amused smile on Dan's face. Inside, antique fishing gear mounted on cedar paneling gave the place a homey feel. The fireplace scented the air with wood smoke, a vast improvement over the stench of fish that had permeated the only bait and tackle shop he'd ever visited. He scuffed his shoes on a thick, bristly doormat, glancing at the customers who browsed sparkling glass cases. They all looked as if they'd stepped off the pages of *GQ* and, knowing he fit right in, Dan drew an easy breath before stepping onto an acre of tongue-and-groove.

"Welcome to On The Fly," called a wizened man whose pumpkin-colored shirt sported multiple pockets.

He rounded a sales counter, the hem of loose khaki shorts flapping above his skinny knees.

"Nice place you have here." Dan traded smiles with the man who closed the gap between them.

"We like it. My name's Sam," the clerk answered. His grin widened. "Your first visit?"

"Yeah," Dan said agreeably. "I need to hire a fly fishing guide. Who's your best?"

Sam threw a glance toward the back of the store where a door swung closed. "You just missed the owner. If you're looking for number one, you'll have to see her, but she went upstairs, uh, home for a bit."

A woman fly fishing guide? What were the odds there were two of them in the same town? A warm feeling spread from the pit of Dan's stomach. Half hoping he was wrong, he asked, "Does she have a boy about four or five?"

"Ay-yup. That'd be Adam," Sam said. He squinted and his chin tilted to the side, pulling the rest of his face down with it. "You're the guy who cost Adam his red fish, aren't you?"

"You got me. I'm Dan Hamilton," he said, offering Sam a handshake. Behind his smile, he wondered if he'd wasted a trip to the store. The cocky blonde's ties to Phelps Cove ran deeper than he thought if she'd mentioned their run-in to her clerk.

Sam angled them toward a side room where wooden grids held swarms of bug-shaped lures. His pale blue eyes narrowed until Dan felt certain the man had lasered off a slice of his skin to put under a microscope.

"Jess's had it rough since Tom died," he said, his voice a slow, careful drawl. "You might be better off if I helped you."

Dan stilled. He hadn't even considered that the guide

might be a widow, her son as fatherless as he was. He eyed the clerk whose rigid stance now made sense. There'd be no getting past the protective guard without a good explanation, and he had one.

"I need to learn enough about fly fishing so I don't embarrass myself on a trip to the Caribbean with my business partners in April."

This latest information didn't go down as well as he'd hoped because the man fired off another round of questions.

"You from around here? What do you and your business partners do for a living?"

Dan pretended interest in a display of long-sleeved shirts. He hadn't expected an inquisition, but the sour expression on Sam's face told him he'd better pony up a good account of himself if he hoped to hire the guide he needed. He slipped one hand into a pants pocket and shifted his weight to the opposite leg.

"I grew up in the southern end of the county. Attended Melbourne High." He eased back on the tight control he normally kept over his own accent until his syllables softened and the vowels stretched out. "After med school at UF, I set up practice near the hospital. It's going well enough."

Sam didn't back down an inch.

"A doctor, huh?" he said. "You sure you ain't a builder? Want to put them fancy condos all along the river?"

Dan managed a straight face long enough to say, "I'm pretty sure I'm a thoracic surgeon."

The answer earned a barely suppressed snort, followed by an invitation to look around while Sam let Jess know she had a visitor. Now that he'd passed the test, Dan had second thoughts. Though the idea of spending time with the spunky guide held a certain appeal, he wasn't sure he wanted to sign up for lectures on the sanctity of Phelps Cove.

But surely they could be adult about the disputed property. He wasn't planning to marry the woman. They didn't even run in the same social circles. All he needed was the right equipment and someone to teach him a few rudimentary skills. The rest he could manage on his own.

His plan made, he stepped behind a counter to run his finger down the spine of a handsome fly rod made of tapered graphite. The finish felt like silk and he lifted it, intending to test its balance the way all the fly fishing books said to do. He imagined himself standing in a river somewhere with Jess Cofer at his side. She'd be surprised at how well a novice mastered the techniques of fly fishing and offer to—

"If you want to keep those fingers, buster, put that rod down slowly and back away."

"Excuse me?" The rod rattled onto its rack and, bristling at a welcome that wasn't exactly what he'd envisioned, he turned to face her. A corona of untamed curls surrounded her flushed cheeks.

Whatever had upset her this time, only a fool could miss how passionately she felt about it. And he was no fool—not that she'd give him a chance to prove it.

"You make a habit of showing up where you don't belong. First where my son and I were fishing. Now here. What are you doing behind my counter?"

"There's no no-trespassing sign." He pointed to the bare wall above his head.

Her frown deepened. "There isn't?"

She swept past, stabbing one finger at a miniscule brass plate screwed into a cedar shingle.

"Huh," he grunted. He'd been so entranced by the workmanship, he hadn't considered the rod might be off-limits. He tried to scrutinize the inscription, but Jess brushed past him, leaving the scent of sunshine mixed with citrus in her wake. His head filling with another breath of her, he bent down to read, *Sweet Baby Blue by T. Cofer.*

Maybe Jess wasn't her first name. The odds were against him, but he still had to ask, "You made this?"

"Built," she corrected. She whipped a soft cloth from her back pocket and ran it down the navy-blue spine. "Fly fishermen *build* rods. And no," she said, her voice thinning, "my husband built this one." Her eyes riveted on the graphite, she buffed until every trace of finger-prints disappeared and made him wait while she settled the rod onto its holder. Her back was still turned to him, and he strained to hear as she murmured, "On The Fly was Tom's pride and joy. He loved nothing more than spending time with his customers. It was their idea to hang Blue in the showroom."

Her statement rankled him in ways he didn't want to consider. He might not be ready for a wife and family, but once he was, they'd take top billing. He stopped short of saying as much. Jess might not be the right woman for him, but disparaging her late husband wouldn't convince the guide to give him lessons. To do that, he needed to find her good side—if she had one—and get on it.

He choked down his pride and summoned a disarming grin.

"I think we got off on the wrong foot. Any chance for a do-over?"

He could see Jess fight it, but he suspected a softer side lay beneath all her bluster, and when one corner of her mouth quirked into a half smile, it convinced him he was right.

"Okay then," she said. "Rewind, and take two."

He spun away, careful this time to keep his hands at his sides until he heard Jess say, "I was told you wanted to see me, Dan?"

"Hamilton," he finished. Giving his best British spy impersonation, he rotated smoothly. "Dan Hamilton."

The cool look he had intended to send her way faltered when a pair of full lips curved sweetly into a smile that kicked his heart rate up a notch. He nudged his focus up along with it, drinking in his first good look at a face he'd only seen when she was peeved with him. A face that should never hide behind floppy hats and sunglasses, he decided when eyes the color of a moonless night took his own captive. He met her stare until her thick lashes dropped down to dust the tops of her cheeks. Though the blink provided an opportunity to look elsewhere, he refused to wander far from smooth, sun-drenched cheeks and shoulder-length hair.

And what he saw, he liked.

She extended her hand. "*Dr.* Hamilton, right? It's a pleasure to meet you," she said. She paused a half beat before adding, "Again."

He took her smaller hand in his, surprised at first by the strength of her grip, a feeling that quickly turned to amazement when warmth pulsed from her fingertips straight up his arm and into his chest.

"The pleasure's all mine," he said, meaning every word far more than the platitude implied.

But she must not have felt what he did, because she gave a very businesslike nod to Baby Blue—now safely ensconced in its rack—and asked, "Pretty, isn't it?"

He relinquished his hold on her fingers. "A beauty,"

he agreed. It took more effort than he thought it should to make sure they were on the same topic.

"Perfectly balanced," she added.

She pointed toward the plaque, and another breath of spicy citrus filled the air between them.

"It's one of Tom's best. We opened On The Fly right after college. Our plan was for him to run the store and build custom rods for select clients."

He noted the wistful quality of her voice and saw the fine tremble that ran along her clenched jaw.

"And your role?" he asked.

"I would take them fishing, of course," she answered. "I studied marine life in college so it seemed like the perfect fit. Plus, I loved being out on the water instead of cooped up inside all day, while Tom lived for the next sale. But things didn't work out the way we planned, and he died." Her eyes overly bright, she finished with a sigh.

"That had to be tough," he offered. "How long's it been?"

"Five years." She shrugged. "After Adam was born, I took over the shop until he started kindergarten. Now that he's in school, I'm rebuilding my client list." She stopped herself, the way his patients sometimes did when they realized they were telling him more than they'd intended. "So, what brings you here on a rainy Wednesday afternoon?"

"Nothing nefarious," he deadpanned. The thought of spending two minutes without arguing with the beautiful guide held a certain appeal. He checked his watch. One down. One more, and maybe they'd have a chance.

He tugged his PDA from its holster and scrolled to a list he was certain she would appreciate. Since appearance was important to his new business partners, he'd chosen the best money could buy, right down to the custom-built rod he planned to order for himself. He watched Jess's face, anticipating her approval.

Jess quashed his pride with a challenging look. "Get this off the internet, did ya?"

"What makes you think that?" he blustered. A second look at her unimpressed expression told him he'd be better off to 'fess up and admit that, in the days since the poker party, he'd scoured the web and every fly fishing book he could lay his hands on.

Jess's skepticism showed in the slight narrowing of her eyes. "Half this stuff is only good in the rocky creeks of North Carolina or Tennessee. The other half is just plain wrong. You don't know much about fishing around here, do you?"

"Nope," he admitted. There was no sense lying about it. If he convinced her to help him, she'd discover his total lack of experience anyway. He summoned up his best smile. "I was actually hoping you would teach me." Thousands of people went fishing every day. He was certain he could master the sport in a few short lessons.

"Yeah. No," she said, managing to raise and smash his hopes in the same breath. "There are a few things we'd need to clear up before I'd take you on as a client."

"Such as?"

"There's the little matter of our meeting the other day."

"Yes, about that…" He took his time. One minute and thirty seconds had passed. What he had to say about his business at Phelps Cove wouldn't get them past the two-minute mark.

Before he answered, Jess's glance drifted past a display of fly-tying materials to a customer who had edged close enough to listen in on their conversation. "I think we'd better take this out of earshot," she stage-whispered. "Let's go to my office."

When Jess headed toward the back of the store without so much as a glance in his direction, Dan shook his head in near disbelief at the guide's prickly nature. At the hospital, staff jumped to carry out his orders. In his office, everyone from the nurses to the janitor respected his wishes and his space. Bantering with the slim blonde offered a rare challenge, one he enjoyed almost more than he was willing to admit, but staying on her good side wouldn't be easy. Especially, if she refused to budge on the issue of Phelps Cove.

Not that he had any doubt he could change her mind.

Once she learned how he intended to use his profits from The Aegean, a single mom like Jess was bound to give her support. He followed her swaying hips into an office where fishing vests in plastic bags spilled from boxes piled on the lone guest chair. While Jess brushed aside papers and ledgers so she could perch on one corner of an old oak desk, he gave up on the idea of clearing his own place to sit. He was eager to put the land business behind them so they could move on to more pressing matters—schedules and prices for her guide service.

"If you're a doctor like Sam says you are, what were you doing on the Phelps property this weekend?" she asked.

He was on the verge of explaining when his gaze stalled on a large poster that seemed out of place in the sea of fishing paraphernalia. Against a forest background, a black bear rose on its hind legs, one paw beckoning.

Only You Can Protect Our Environment, the caption said. Join POE Today. Save the World for Tomorrow.

Hundreds of photos peppered the walls. Some were so old they'd faded, their edges curled. Boxes of supplies filled every nook, and paperwork spilled off every conceivable surface. From the look of things, the busy woman hadn't cleared the office since her husband's death. He told himself the poster on the wall was probably another leftover.

Nevertheless, he felt as if he was venturing onto treacherous ground when he asked, "Your husband was active in the environmental movement?"

Jess studied the shopping list on his PDA while she answered. "No, that baby's all mine. Why?"

Dan took a quick step away from the bookcase. If Bryce or Jack so much as suspected him of involvement with the antidevelopment activists, they'd boot him out of The Aegean group before the next poker party.

He gave Jess a rueful glance. As much as he'd enjoy having the beautiful fly fisher for a teacher, her involvement with POE put her off-limits. It was time to cut his losses.

"My friends and I plan to develop the property. It's perfect for what we have in mind."

AND HERE SHE'D THOUGHT THE DOCTOR might be a decent guy. Jess splayed her fingers over her clenched stomach and figured the odds of that weren't good.

"That's impossible," she argued. She'd worked too hard for too long to let anyone turn the pristine wilderness into a glorified parking lot. "Phelps Cove will be a protected habitat before summer."

"According to your sources." Her would-be client added a dismissive shrug. "Mine tell me differently."

"What sources?" She let her eyes narrow into a look that produced immediate results whenever she focused it on Adam. "I thought you were a doctor."

"I am," he nodded. "My specialty is thoracics. I'm a surgeon."

One of those. Not only full of himself, but so rich he probably grew up thinking the U.S. Mint existed to put silver on his table. His profession put him in league with men like the ones Tom had taken fishing on the day he died.

She gave him a long, careful appraisal, noting the fair complexion of a man who spent most of his time indoors. She'd swallow a hand-tied minnow if he made a practice of tramping through the woods. His list was clearly meant to impress, but she'd steer him away from custom-mades with their higher price tags. Her actions might cost On The Fly a few bucks, or even send Dan to a competitor, but it'd be worth every penny if it made the dangerously handsome doctor walk out her door and never return.

"All right, Dr. Hamilton." She rose from her desk with a determined professionalism. "Let's see what we can do to get you set up for fly fishing. You have wading boots on your list and we have some nice ones on sa—"

"I saw what I wanted on the display by the door," Dan interrupted.

"We have some nice ones on sale this week," she continued as if he hadn't spoken. The finely tooled leather boots were exactly what she did *not* want to sell him. "You need a pair made of durable rubber. No matter how you treat them, they'll last a lifetime."

Dan's frown was enough to let her know she was on the right track.

"I did my research. I chose the best brands, the best styles," he objected.

"And you did a great job," she said with the tiniest dollop of sarcasm. "But the way we take care of our equipment is a huge part of the fly fishing culture. If I sell you something that won't hold up under the heat, humidity and corrosive salt we have in Florida, it reflects badly on me. I can't afford to have you walking around in broken-down boots and telling people you bought them at On The Fly." She thrust her hands onto her hips. "Unless *my* reputation doesn't matter to you?"

She could see she'd struck home by the way Dan's eyes fell to his Sketchers. Tasting victory, she pushed harder. "How much fishing have you done?"

"None," he answered. "I haven't had the inclination until recently." Arms crossed, he leaned one shoulder against the wall.

Though his gaze rose to meet hers, she had him on the defensive. With just one more shove, two at the most, he would walk away....

"Not even as a kid?" she challenged. "Every kid goes fishing." It was as much a part of growing up as baseball, hot dogs and apple pie.

"Not me," he answered without blinking. "None of my foster parents had money for stuff like that."

His *foster* parents?

So much for her theory that a coddled and sheltered childhood had led Dan straight into one of the country's most lucrative professions. She wanted to ask how he'd done it, how he'd managed, not only to survive, but to excel. But he had steered the conversation into waters that gave her the single-mom shivers, and her head filled with the sort of "What if?" questions that were hard to banish. It was time to quit giving the man a hard time and move on.

"Okay, you win," she said as fast as she could get the words out of her mouth. "Let's go get those boots."

He scuffed a shoe against one of the floor planks. "No, you're right," he said. "We'll do it your way."

On The Fly's wealthy patrons did not compromise, especially once she'd given in to their demands. Dan Hamilton was full of surprises, and Jess locked her jaw so her mouth wouldn't drop open. As eager as she was to rid the shop of his disturbing presence, she conceded that she might've been a little hasty in lumping her newest customer in with her most pretentious clientele. With the chip on her shoulder on a crash diet, they spent the next hour in a pleasant give-and-take, settling on rubber boots to protect his feet from stingrays and a broad-brimmed hat to keep the sun off his neck.

Their cease-fire ended at a rack of expensive rods.

"I can't sell you those," she said when he stopped to eye a rod that would pay Adam's tuition in a fancy private school for a month.

"Look, Jess. I've taken most of your suggestions, but I want this." Dan reached for an eight-weight done in forest-green.

She studied his selection. Its perfect balance would make the graphite feel as light as a feather in his hand. It was exactly the right choice for trout fishing along the Indian River. At a shade under two grand, the rod was also too expensive for a beginner who would probably snap it in half on his first outing.

"That's not the right one for you," she insisted.

Intending to draw his hand away from the rack, she reached out. The instant her fingers touched his skin, her body responded, sending a bolt of heat up her arm. She yanked her hand back and sucked in a breath, struggling to find the rest of her argument.

"If it's the money you're worried about, don't." He flipped over a small white tag on the grip, barely glancing at the price. "It's within my budget."

Of course, it was. He was a surgeon, after all.

"Let me lend you a rod for now. Once you've mastered it, you can come back and spend a small fortune."

"A practice rod?" Dan seemed to mull over the idea, his fingers trailing from his choice as he turned to face her. His voice dropped. "Does it come with lessons?"

Other men had given her that same look and she hadn't even felt a spark, but Dan's searching gaze seared her to the core. She couldn't afford to get burned.

"Sorry. I'm a guide. I don't teach."

When his warm and inviting eyes grew frosty, Jess was surprised how much she hated seeing that spark ice over. She took a mental step back to evaluate.

Of course she was attracted to him—what girl in her right mind wouldn't be? With looks like his, he could charm a fish out of the water without a rod or a reel. She took a speculative peek at his narrow hips and impossibly long legs. If Dan ever changed his stance on Phelps Cove, she might even reconsider Sam's advice on dating.

So, how had he ended up on the wrong side of such an important issue?

As impossible as it seemed, the man said he'd never gone fishing. He'd never experienced the pleasures of being on the water. He'd never felt the thrill of setting a hook or making the perfect cast. Maybe all he needed was to see how much fun it could be and he'd change his mind about ruining the best fishing grounds in the area.

And who better to teach him than herself?

"I give an orientation for new fly fishers on the second Saturday of the month," she suggested as casually as her racing heart would allow. "If you're interested, you should come."

The invitation brought the light back to Dan's eyes. "Maybe," he allowed, smiling. "Maybe I will."

Jess made sure to keep her distance during the rest of his shopping foray, and soon she was ringing up his not-insignificant purchases, handing him a well-used rod, and guiding him to the door. She lingered at the glass, mesmerized by the view until Dan reached his car.

"He seems like a nice enough guy."

"Sam!" The manager's sudden presence at her elbow made her jump. "You startled me." She aimed her chin toward the parking lot. "Yeah, he's okay."

"Did I hear right? He wanted to buy that Sage." Sam hooked a thumb over one shoulder to the rack of expensive rods. "And you talked him out of it?"

Dan's car pulled onto main road.

"He'll be back." She turned away from the door and faced her manager. "For one thing, he signed up for the next orientation class."

The way Sam's sparse eyebrows rose, she could tell he found that hard to believe.

"It's true," she insisted.

"Do you think that was a smart thing to do?"

She shrugged. Smart or not, Dan Hamilton would have to prove himself. She was no carefree, single gal to be taken in by a ready grin and a broad chest. She had responsibilities and, no matter how attractive she found him, there were certain things she needed to know about the man before she considered spending time with

him—even if all they did was fish. A week from Saturday, Dan would face his first test.

"Jess." Sam shook his head. "That man deserves
better. For that matter, the way you've been treating all
our customers could stand some improvement."

She felt her face flush. "You are so—"

Sam folded his arms across his chest. The lines on
his face hardened.

"You really want to go there?" he challenged.

She managed to stop herself before she said something she didn't mean and, from the look on the older
man's face, wouldn't be able to take back.

"—Right," she conceded with a sigh. She shook her
head. "I don't know what's gotten into me, but you're
right. I'll call..." Her voice trailed off as the phone
beside the cash register rang. On her way to answer it,
she grumbled, "I'll call him and cancel."

But Bob Richards was on the line and, from the sound
of his voice, Jess sensed trouble.

"Have you read today's paper?" asked the head of
POE. "The Editorial page?"

"No." Adam had dawdled over breakfast which, in
turn, had delayed her arrival at On The Fly. She had
bypassed the usual coffee with Sam and gone straight
to work. "Is there something I should know?"

"There's a piece in there about our funding. The
author makes a compelling argument for development.
He asks why the state is spending money on land it can't
use when the economy has forced us to slash education
and road budgets. The way he puts it, it sounds like the
POE is robbing the schools in order to build another
park."

"Not true," Jess protested. "The money for Phelps
Cove comes from a different revenue stream altogether."

Once the state owned the land, POE would manage it using bond money that had to be spent on protected habitats.

"You and I know that, but most people may not understand the difference. I'm concerned." Bob was headed for the capitol where he'd poll support for POE and do everything he could to make sure it was rock solid. Meanwhile, he wanted Jess to draft a rebuttal for the paper.

"Will do," she agreed after they'd discussed strategies another minute or two. As she headed to her office, other concerns faded into the background while her thoughts narrowed in on protecting Phelps Cove.

Chapter Six

A few minutes before nine on a cool Saturday morning, Dan squared his shoulders against the car's seat back.

"Let the games begin," he whispered, spinning the wheel to make the final turn toward On The Fly.

He loved a good challenge, and Jess Cofer promised to be a doozy. She'd start off giving instructions, but he was certain he wouldn't need much help. He'd read the books, after all, and might even be able to show her a thing or two. Though there was always the possibility he'd mess up on purpose. If he did, would she slip her arms around him to demonstrate?

He thought it might be worth finding out until one look at the circus-like atmosphere of the crowded parking lot told him his rival for Phelps Cove had pulled a fast one. The white tents were new since his visit ten days ago. So were the meaty smells and smoke billowing from charcoal grills. He spotted Sam beside a makeshift gate that led to the field alongside the store and headed toward the manager who had exchanged his pumpkin-colored shirt for the same model in bright blue.

"Hey, Doc. Didn't expect to see you today." Sam handed a short fly rod to an even shorter boy and gave the child's father a disposable fishing vest.

"This is the orientation class, isn't it?" He nodded toward the freshly mown field. "Jess pretty much said it was mandatory before she'd sell me the rod I like."

"She was supposed to call." Sam removed his baseball cap and ran a hand through his sparse hair. "I don't suppose she told ya the class is mostly for kids?"

"She must have forgotten to mention that part," Dan answered, sparing the men and children lined up in the grass an amused glance.

"Guess so. You gonna stick around?"

He nodded. No small effort had been required to clear the day's schedule. "I think I will."

Sam's brow furrowed as he studied an array of toy-size rods. "None of these'll work for you. I'll get 'cha one from inside, if you don't mind waiting a minute or two."

"I have the one Jess lent me in the car," Dan offered. Lately, his schedule had been so tight, he hadn't even had a chance to try it out.

"That ol' thing? Nah," Sam scoffed. "I can do better than that." He turned away. "Adam, will you watch things?"

Jess's son nodded from his perch atop a split-rail fence. "Yes, sir," he called. After Sam hurried off to get the appropriate equipment, the boy shot him a glance, little fingers visibly tightening their grip on the top slat.

"Hey, Adam," he called. "Mind if I join you?"

He took the boy's shrug for permission and made his way to the fence. "So, what's happening here today? Your mom hold these classes often?"

Adam's focus on the people in the field never wavered. "Not all the time, but a lot. This one's for kids and their dads." He pointed to the closest pair. "They're gonna learn to fly fish together."

The wistful note in the child's voice twisted something in Dan's gut. He cleared his throat. "You fish with your mom. That's pretty special. I hear she's the best."

"Yeah, she's pretty good for a mom," Adam nodded. "But sometimes, I wish I had a dad." As if he were imparting a very important piece of information, he added, "Mine's in heaven."

Dan looked around for help. He had no idea what to say next. With Sam nowhere to be seen, he went with the truth. "I don't have a dad, either. Guess that makes you and me sort of the same."

"Really?" Adam's eyes grew wide. He thrust up his hand and let it hang in midair.

Dan eyed the child's one-handed grip on the fence rail when the rail shifted beneath Adam's weight, but the boy adjusted his position without losing his balance.

"Hey," Adam said frowning. "You're supposed to give me a high-five 'cause we're the same."

"Whoops." Dan slapped the boy's hand and grinned, realizing Adam was as agile as a cat. "Thanks for reminding me, tiger."

Adam leaned forward far enough to check the empty space at Dan's side. "How can you take the class if you didn't bring someone with you?"

The question presented a welcome chance to steer the conversation in a different direction, and he took it.

"I think your mom was pulling a trick on me," he said, pointing toward Jess. In the shorts and shirt he'd come to think of as her work uniform, the woman was everywhere at once, tanned legs counting off a dozen feet or more between each father-child duo, toned arms placing hula hoops on the ground in front of the pairs.

When she stopped to tug the ponytail of a dark-haired girl and smiled in response to some comment from the child's father, a feeling he couldn't identify stirred in his chest. "Do you think she'd do that?"

Adam's mouth scrunched to one side as he gave the matter serious thought. "I think she did," he said at last. He peeked up from beneath a wide hat brim. "You should trick her right back."

"Hmm." Dan rubbed his chin. "That's a good idea." One he was all in on until he saw Jess's stricken expression when she looked his way.

"I'm so sorry," she mouthed.

That strange feeling rustled through him again. He couldn't help smiling and giving her a nod. In return, Jess waved him over. "Class is about to start. Grab a rod and join us."

He'd taken a step or two before he realized that his departure would leave Adam all alone. "I'd be the only one out there without someone," he said to the boy. "Do you think…" He hesitated. "I mean, I know you're already good at this, but it would make me feel a lot better if you'd be my partner. If it's okay with your mom, that is."

The speed at which Adam scrambled down off the fence told Dan he'd been right to ask. And even though she tugged the ubiquitous floppy hat so low it kept her face in shadow, he sensed he'd pleased Jess, as well. Adam grabbed one of the kiddie rods from the table and they took their place on the field with everyone else.

"Welcome to On The Fly's orientation class," Jess began at once, "where you'll learn all about strange words like *wooly bugger* and *caddis fly*." Tipping her hat back, she scrunched her face and held her nose until every kid laughed.

"Fly fishing is a lot of fun," she continued. "You might have to practice a little to get it right, but today, we're going to start by making a cast into a hula hoop." She aimed her own much longer rod toward the plastic circles. "When we're done, we'll have hot dogs and ice cream. How does that sound?"

Though he didn't need the promised treats, Dan added his own cheers to those of the rest of the class. While they waited for Sam, he held the skinny child's rod the way Adam showed him. His fingers practically dwarfed it as he pulled line from the reel and let it puddle at his feet. His long arms made handling the short pole so easy that, when Jess walked them through the motions of their first cast, his little blob of yarn was the only one that landed inside the hula hoop. Under Adam's careful direction, he repeated the process until, on his fourth or fifth try, he glanced over one shoulder to see his young partner sitting cross-legged on the ground, pulling at a clump of grass.

"What's up, Adam?" he asked.

The boy's thin shoulders rose and fell in a way that made Dan search for a reason. It didn't take long to find one. Up and down the line of parents and children, his was the only recalcitrant aide. Then again, he was the only "student" who didn't really need the help. He scuffed a foot through the grass and deliberately tangled his line on the next cast.

"Would ya look at that," he exclaimed. "What do I do now?"

He turned a helpless look on the boy who was already scrambling to his feet. Adam no sooner sorted out the knotted line than Dan tangled it again, a move that elicited laughter, and a fair amount of teasing, from the child. He continued his antics until Sam reappeared.

"There you go, Doc," said the slightly out of breath manager. "This one's rigged and ready."

The seven-foot rod Sam placed in his hands was considerably less wieldy than the three-footer Dan'd been using. When a gust of air blew his fly off course, he learned that his new equipment, unlike the kiddie poles with their blobs of yarn, came armed with a real hook. A hook that apparently had a mind of its own and absolutely did not want to land inside the hula hoop. Smart enough to stay out of range, Adam coached from the sidelines.

Heat rose above Dan's shirt collar when every one of a dozen attempts sailed beyond the circle.

"Ready to give up?" Jess asked. "Let everybody have their hot dogs and ice cream?"

Though a quick glance told him all the kids had hit their targets and now lined the fence, Jess's teasing smile spurred him to take another try or two. He stopped to remove the hook from his brand new Polo shirt.

"You guys go ahead," he answered. "I'll keep at it."

"No one eats till everyone eats," Jess quipped loud enough for all to hear.

With her standing there, one hand propped on a cocked hip, he fumbled another cast.

"You're doing everything right," she coached. "Just get the slack out of the line and you'll do great."

When she put it that way, it sounded simple enough. It took another two tries before he found the rhythm, but once he did, Jess's wide grin made the extra effort worthwhile. The accomplishment made him feel prouder than it should have, and he gave a bow. A cheer soon rose from the fence.

"Let's eat," Dan suggested.

No one needed a second invitation. As he cut

across the field with the rest of the group, Jess fell in beside him.

"That was a nice thing you did for Adam," she said.

"We had fun together." Dan watched the boy run to catch up with some others his own age. Though there were more differences than similarities between his past and Adam's present, he'd been the kid with no dad, and could relate. Maybe he could talk to Jess about it more over lunch. "I think I've worked up an appetite. How 'bout you?"

"Sorry, but I'm working." Jess fanned a handful of business cards and moved off, stalling his attempt to get to know her better.

Adam and a couple of other boys were talking at a corner table so he grabbed a dog and a place in the shade while Jess made the rounds handing out flyers to promote her guide service. Casting had proven more of a challenge than he'd anticipated. If he was going to master it—and everything else he needed to learn before the trip to Belize—he'd need more than a lesson or two. He glanced at Jess at the opposite end of the tent. She was a challenge, too. At least, she'd apologized, something he hadn't been certain she was capable of doing.

"I'm free on Wednesday afternoons," he said when she worked her way close enough. "Put me down for ten half days."

"Yeah?" Jess raised an eyebrow. She shook her head. "No."

DAN HAMILTON CONTINUED TO SURPRISE her. He expected to hire her as a private tutor? The idea was ludicrous...and too scary to contemplate. Even if she had the inclination, she didn't have time for killer smiles and boy-next-door looks. Not with On The Fly to run. Not with Adam to love and raise in her single-parent household. Not with Dan threatening to clear-cut Phelps Cove and turn it into...what? They never had gotten around to discussing his plans.

Confidence showed in his dark eyes. She wondered how far she'd have to push before he gave up and looked for another instructor.

"No," she repeated. Fighting to steady herself, she added, "I'm not available on Wednesdays."

His smile faltered. "That's the only day I have free."

"Guess you'll have to find another guide then."

A throat-clearing growl stopped her from saying more. Her frown deepened when Sam edged past a crowded picnic table wearing a look that was downright thunderous. Before she could manage more than a quick, "Excuse me a minute," the man steered her away from prying ears.

"What are you doing?" he hissed. "I thought you wanted to build clientele for your guide service. How is turning down the doc gonna do that?"

She shrugged and tried for wide-eyed innocence. "He's a novice. Doesn't know one end of a fly rod from the other. There'd be a lot more teaching than guiding involved. Besides, I work the sales floor on Wednesdays. It's your day off."

"I'll switch then. We need the income. You and I both know the shop's been losing ground."

"Don't remind me," she groaned as the weight of the world settled on her shoulders. On The Fly was as much Adam's future as it had been Tom's dream. Not only that, but people she cared for, people like Sam and her other employees, depended on the shop for their livelihoods.

She couldn't afford to turn away new customers, even if they did pose a threat to something she'd spent years working for.

She beckoned Dan over and summoned her patience when the man took a slug of soda before joining them. "So, what's the verdict?" he asked.

She loved the way his weight shifted as if he were antsy about the answer. As if there weren't fifty other fishing guides within a twenty-mile radius. Any of whom would be glad to take his money and spend whatever day of the week he wanted on the water. If he threw his weight around and went all prima donna on her, she'd even refer him to one or two of them. No matter what it cost her.

"As inconvenient as it is for him, Sam has agreed to switch his days off."

A wide grin broke across Dan's face.

"But…" She paused.

Tension etched his smile lines a little deeper. "But?"

"It has to be mornings, not afternoons."

"Now, wait a minute Jess," Sam interrupted. "What's it matter what time you take the doc fishing?"

Jess silenced him with a smug look. "Thunderstorms. You know we get them late in the day." Satisfied, she swung to challenge her potential client. "Does that interfere with your schedule, too?"

Dan's brown eyes bore into hers until she read the truth in them. He was on to her ploy. Afternoon storms weren't routine until the summer heat and humidity rolled in.

"Mornings are actually reserved for patient records and updates," he said.

"That settles it, then." Jess's breath seeped across her

lips, leaving her more deflated than the victor in a battle should feel.

Dan juggled the soda bottle in his hands and leaned back. "But I suppose I could change things around. Unless you have another excuse for why that won't work for you?"

She'd have bet her favorite fly rod that he didn't have a compromising bone in his sturdy frame. And she'd have been wrong. She hated to be wrong. But in this case, she thought it might work to her advantage. If Dan was willing to compromise on some of the little things, she'd use their lessons to change his mind about the big things, too.

Things like Phelps Cove.

DAN TIPPED HIS CHAIR BACK and surveyed the littered remains of Sunday dinner. The enormous bowl of mashed potatoes had been scraped clean. Someone had taken the last of the gravy. A few gummy slices of okra were all that was left of the vegetables. Barbecue sauce still scented the air, but the only sign of a mountain of grilled chicken were the tiny pools of grease that dotted a platter. If he looked closely, he could see a chip in a bowl here, a crack in a plate there. Not that any of the young men crowded around the table would notice. Ask any one of them, and they'd say full bellies, their own room, safety—those were the things that mattered.

He grinned at Maddy as, one by one, those who had eaten their fill darted quick glances at a cuckoo clock so time-worn the bird had disappeared long before Dan had downed his first mouthful at this trestle table. In all that time, the house rules hadn't changed. At least ten minutes of conversation followed every meal, and his foster mom had been known to tack on an extra half hour if she decided people were in too big a hurry to leave.

"I'm right. You'll see." Chris, the latest addition to the household and a scrappy character, tossed an uneaten dinner roll at Sean. "It's gonna be Orlando and L.A. in the play-offs for sure."

Sean backhanded the food missile. "The Celtics and the Lakers, man. The Magic'll go down in flames."

As conversation veered toward the basketball game on TV that afternoon, Dan leaned in to speak with Glen. "Have you had a chance to think about the kinds of services we need to provide? I mean, beside the clinic we already talked about."

Glen's brow furrowed. "What's the rush? Connections House is, what, five years down the road?"

"Maybe not," Dan answered. "Assuming we break ground for The Aegean this spring, we should start seeing profits within a year. Eighteen months at the outside. If our projections are right, I'll shave the time frame for the house down to two, maybe three, years."

"If everything goes according to plan. You don't even have a contract on the land yet, do you?"

"There's no reason to expect a delay." Unless Jess Cofer and POE threw a last-minute Hail Mary. According to the guys at the poker table, there wasn't much chance of that happening.

"I still say it's too early."

Dan rubbed his forehead. Glen's response was always the same. Too early to settle on how many kids they could manage. Too early to decide whether a class in personal checking or basic grocery shopping was more important. Too early for staffing commitments. If he didn't know better, he'd think the man who ran an unof-

ficial home for older foster kids opposed his plans for
a larger, better one.

"Do you have a problem…" he began.

"Mr. Glen," Sean interrupted. "Is it okay if I take
Regina outside to shoot some hoops?"

Glen's attention shifted to his wife at the opposite
end of the table. "That all right with you, Maddy?"

With a sip of her tea and a shooing motion, the
woman who shared the burden of caring for six gradu-
ates of the foster care system signaled her permission.
"Okay, gentlemen. You know the drill. There's work
to be done before that TV goes on. Boys, you clear the
dishes and clean the kitchen. Regina, honey, you can
sweep the floor. Make sure you push back all the chairs
and get under the table real good."

Belligerent posturing had greeted the same request
the last time Regina had joined them for a Sunday
meal, but today she simply shot a questioning look at
her brother. At Sean's barely perceptible nod, the girl's
head bobbed.

"Yes, ma'am," she said quietly.

The response brought amused smiles to the lips
of the adults. Less than a week after moving in with
Carol Shea, the child was blossoming. Dan didn't know
who was more pleased about that—Sean, Regina or
himself.

Chairs scraped noisily against scarred hardwood as
the young men, adults and the lone girl pushed away
from the table. Dan stood with the rest of the "boys" and
began clearing dishes. He might be a doctor, might live
on his own in a condo ten miles and a lifetime away, but
everyone who sat down to Sunday dinner at the Hollises'
helped with the cleanup afterward. Not that he minded
the chance to find out who had a new girlfriend and who

didn't. Who struggled with math and who excelled at sports.

Seconds after the last dish was stored in the cabinet, people scattered. Pre-game coverage quickly blared from the television. Sean, who preferred playing basketball to watching the sport, headed outside with Regina. Dan glanced at the young men sprawled across every threadbare couch and chair in sight, and followed the pair out the door. On his way to his car for the fly rod Jess had lent him, he stopped at the front porch swing.

"Want to come along?" he asked Glen.

The older man only smiled and lifted Maddy's hand in his, and Dan moved on.

Water babbled down a pile of gray coquina rocks just past the pond Glen and some of the boys had dug in one corner of the backyard. Listening to the rhythmic *thump, thump, thump* of the basketball coming from another home-improvement project, a half-court on the other side of the house, Dan took a few practice casts and kept at it until he could hit the pond from twenty paces.

"Good one, Dr. Dan," he heard Regina's soft voice exclaim later.

"Thanks." He aimed a grin at the girl who sat cross-legged, well beyond the reach of his fly line. "Get tired of basketball?"

"A couple of the other guys—Jose and the one with the cross tattoo—they're playing with Sean."

An occasional grunt accompanied the faster-paced sound of the basketball bouncing against asphalt. "That'd be Chris." He sent another cast toward the pond. The fly splashed softly into the water. "Neither of them is as good as your brother, but together, they'll give him a workout."

He reeled in and, aiming to improve his reach, backed up a step.

Regina tilted her head to one side. "I've never seen a fishing pole like that one. Why do you wave it around so much?"

He let the butt of the rod rest on the ground and explained a little of what he'd gleaned about the sport. "Want to try?" he finished.

Regina gave him a doubtful look. "Nah, that's all right. I'd probably get it all knotted up."

An old hand at insecurity, he recognized it when he heard it. "I've done that. More than once," he answered. He held the rod out to her. "Here. Your turn."

Regina rose to her feet with an easy grace, but shuffled forward like a timid old lady. She swung a look around the yard, probably making sure no one was around to make fun of her. Dan saved the lecture on self-confidence and showed her how to hold the rod before he stepped out of range to walk her through the lessons he'd learned at orientation. To his amazement— and hers—the girl's first attempt sent the fly sailing in the pond's general direction.

"You're a natural," he exclaimed.

Regina's face glowed. "I was lucky. I bet I can't do it again."

But she was already retrieving the line and getting ready to do exactly that. This time, her technique was nearly flawless. The fly landed with a plop not two feet from the spot where it had taken him a dozen tries to place his own cast. He settled down to watch as the girl continued sending the fly where she wanted it to go.

After six or seven perfect throws, she reeled in and walked over to him.

"Is that all there is? It's kinda boring."

"Well." He grinned. "Eventually, the object is to catch a fish. But I'm not using a hook 'cause Mr. Glen wouldn't like it if we killed all his koi." At the girl's puzzled look, he clarified. "The big goldfish."

Silver beads at the ends of her tight braids swayed as Regina handed him the fly rod. "Koi. I like that word."

"I'm taking lessons." He nodded to the rod. "If you and Sean are interested, we can try fishing on Sunday afternoons. I'll show you what I've learned each week."

"You'll put the hooks on? We'll catch fish?" When Dan laughingly agreed, she bit her lip.

"Maybe," Regina said with a wistful glance toward the front of the house where her brother was playing. When a horn beeped, the rhythmic thud of the basketball quieted.

"Regina," called a strong male voice.

"Coming!" she called back. "Thanks, Dr. Dan, but Mrs. Shea said she'd pick me up."

"Hold on a sec." He propped the rod against the rock fountain. "I'll walk with you. Mrs. Shea treating you all right?"

Regina nearly beamed. "I have my own room. There are rules, but that's okay. Sean said if they're fair, you have to follow them."

"Wise advice." He nodded. "You let your brother or me know if there's a problem, though. We're both looking out for you."

"Okay." The girl shrugged. "See ya, Dr. Dan."

He watched as Regina joined her brother who walked her to the car, one long arm draped about her shoulders. When he returned, the boy said, "She sure seems excited about them fly fishing lessons. Maybe you better show me what it's all about before we get together next weekend."

"Glad to," Dan agreed. Before long, he'd repeated what he knew a second time. An hour later, he paid his respects to Glen and Maddy and said his goodbyes to the rest of the boys. He shook his head as he disassembled the fly rod and stored it in his trunk. Two weeks ago, the idea of teaching someone else how to fish would have seemed ridiculous. Now, since it looked as if he had two students, he'd better learn as much as he could, and quickly—Sean and Regina were right on his heels.

Chapter Seven

The air burned frost into Dan's lungs as he stepped from his car into the empty parking lot behind Long Doggers Grill. Icy cold bled through the rubber soles of his boots. After tugging a windbreaker over the shirt he'd purchased at On The Fly, he checked his watch and saw that he was only five minutes early for his first lesson.

He tried telling himself that he'd rolled out of bed before the alarm because he had a lot to learn before the trip to Belize. Truth be told, there was more behind his restless night than he cared to admit. He worried that hiring Jess, a woman fundamentally opposed to his goals, had been a mistake. He'd probably never convince her he had right on his side. And yet…he couldn't resist the opportunity to try to change her mind any more than he could shake the sassy blonde from his thoughts. Before he could settle on an approach, her ancient Chevy truck pulled in beside him.

"Mornin'." Jess's breath and spicy citrus scent plumed through her lowered window.

He looked toward the eastern sky where the sun had yet to make an appearance.

"Barely," he answered, handing across one of two

cups of coffee he'd grabbed at a 7-Eleven. "Cold enough?" He stamped his feet to warm them.

"Best time to catch fish," she countered. "The front pushing through'll make them more active." Turning down his offer of cream or sugar, she slid from the seat and began pulling gear out of the back.

"Seems like an odd place to fish." He'd envisioned wide-open spaces with no one around and swung a questioning look at buildings that towered along the river's edge. Lights already blazed in several of the apartments.

Jess pointed with her free hand. "This was one of my favorite spots when I was a kid."

"Were the condos here then?" He was pretty sure South Beach architecture was new to Brevard County.

"No." She paused for a sip of coffee. "Builders used to leave boggy areas like this one alone. Once land prices rose, someone thought of bringing in fill dirt and putting up high-density housing. No one cared that the runoff killed the sea grass and muddied the water."

"So, why bring me here?" He didn't try to mask his irritation. Jess might be the best fly fishing guide in the area, but a lecture before breakfast was more than he could stomach.

"Don't worry." She faced him, all business and stiff shoulders. "They left one little corner the way it was."

He recognized forced civility when he saw it. Not that it mattered. He could deal with her attitude as long as Jess taught him how to handle a fly rod well enough to impress his new associates and share a few tips with Regina and Sean.

He started for his car and the equipment Jess had lent him. She was busy slipping fly line through guides, but stopped long enough to say, "Leave yours in the car and use this one. It's better suited for this kind of fishing."

Coffee finished, Jess wedged the empty cup into the truck bed and motioned him to do the same. "Ready to get started?"

"Yeah. Let's." He took the gear she handed him and followed her down a narrow path that led between thick brush and manicured grass.

Quiet hung heavily in the air. The lawn gave way to cattails and sea oats tall enough to block the condominiums from view. Jess swiped at spiderwebs as she went, her movements sure and muted. Dan followed suit.

A briny smell rose from the river where the path opened to a narrow, sandy beach. Mist curled in tendrils from the flat surface of black water before turning into a thick fog that hid the opposite shore. Standing there with the sun still beneath the horizon, the sky lighting to shades of gray, Jess's choice of fishing spots made more sense. Even though hundreds of people slept within a quarter mile, he felt as if they were the only two beings on the planet.

At least, he did until a dog-size shape edged out of the fog toward them. He reached for Jess, ready to pull her to safety, but she stepped beyond his grasp.

"Raccoon," she said with an unconcerned look at the sizeable specimen that ambled along the water's edge. "They're nocturnal. He's been out foraging all night and is headed home to sleep."

"Awfully big, isn't he?" He half expected his nature-loving guide to toss a handful of food pellets at the overgrown critter, but other than waiting until the beast ducked into the weeds, she ignored it.

"Yeah," Jess said. "He's probably feasted from

garbage cans his whole life. If there weren't so many houses nearby, he'd have to work harder for his food, and he wouldn't be so fat and lazy."

He cleared his throat. "Look," he said. "You've made your point. I get that we're on opposite sides of the development issue, but for now, how about we stick to fishing?"

Jess set the butt of her rod on the ground. "You may be the client, but I have to tell you—fishing and the environment go hand-in-hand." After yanking several lengths of line from the reel, she changed the subject. "Fly rods come in different lengths and weights for different fishing conditions. This is a nine-foot." The tip barely wavered when she shook the slim graphite. "It's longer and less flexible than anything you've handled before." Doubt and challenge filled her voice. "Let's see what you've got."

Dan let out a long breath. Though he wouldn't complain if the instruction package came with a smile or two, his sharpened skills were sure to impress her. He spilled line for his first cast and was surprised when the loops collapsed behind him. They tangled in the grass. When he finally got enough string in the air to send the fly sailing, the little bugger plummeted to the ground at his feet. Struggling to remember everything he'd learned, he clenched his teeth and reeled in.

"There's the problem. You're trying too hard. Now, don't move till I get in position," Jess cautioned. "Neither of us wants to get hooked today." Stuffing her hair under her hat, she slipped in from behind, cupping his forearms. She gave his arm a reproving shake. "Relax. Don't be so stiff."

But with the press of her soft curves against his back, her breath on his neck, he found it difficult to comply with her request. The slim arms that encircled his waist shoved aside all his carefully marshaled reasons for why being around Jess was a bad idea.

"Small movements here." Her hand on top of his, she rocked the rod back and forth. "Create graceful loops. They fill the line with tension. A quick stroke with the wrist—" her touch had him considering the wisdom of *ever* getting it right "—releases the pressure and it adds distance. Fly fishing is a dance, not a race," she whispered. "Follow my lead."

The invitation conjured up a few places he was certain she didn't mean for him to follow. It took three more tries before he managed to get the line wet without tangling it around their shoulders. When he finally did, she stepped away.

Cold air filled the space where her touch had warmed him. Apparently, her absence also numbed his brain. He turned, risking a quick look into her dark eyes and swallowed to keep from drowning in them. His attraction to the stubborn fly fisher was an unwanted complication, but he had to know if she felt the same thing.

Jess retreated, putting another couple of feet between them. "You're making good progress." Her voice faltered. She cleared her throat. "It's like any new skill—a little frustrating to start." She twisted a loose tendril of hair around one finger, a motion he'd seen her make before when she was uncertain. "You'll get the hang of it."

A loud pop followed by watery thrashing kept him from making the move he was sure he'd regret.

"Fish," Jess said. She pointed to the right. "Cast there."

She didn't have to tell him twice. He scanned the

weeds for the source of the noise and waded into the water to get closer.

"Take your time," she said softly while he worked the fly into the air. "He's just starting to feed."

For once, the cast went where he wanted, but a hard tug nearly jerked the rod straight out of his hands. He tightened his grip and reared back. The line went taut. He fumbled for the knob on the reel and spun it.

Beside him, Jess's calm voice provided encouragement. "Set the hook. Set the hook. Keep the rod tip up."

Though her directions made no sense, pride shot through him at another firm pull from the business end of the line. He reeled faster and had just enough time to wonder why everyone said fishing was so difficult when the fly sailed out of the water all by its lonesome.

Once it dropped back onto the surface, he jiggled the rod tip up and down. The line twitched. His breath fogged the air. Otherwise, nothing. He breathed deep and turned to face Jess. "I'm betting that's not the outcome we wanted."

Her face broke into a smile that swept his disappointment into the dustbin. "No, but it was a good start. You had a fish on the line there for a few seconds."

"Seconds?" He made his best, skeptical face. "Had to be longer than that. Five minutes, at least."

"You're a born fisherman." The corners of her mouth twitched. "You already know how to stretch a story."

He hesitated over the hand she extended. One part of his brain argued that he should keep his distance. The other insisted that Jess was only offering a congratulatory handshake and he'd look foolish if he didn't take it. Determined to resist the latter, he grasped her fingers. But the sudden urge to pull her into his arms shocked him. He whirled so she wouldn't see her effect on him and spun line into the air. The fly snagged the bushes behind them. He jerked to free it.

A soft crack wiped the tight smile from his face. He looked up to see the rod tip dangling from the end of the line.

"Oh, jeez, Jess. I'm sorry."

He braced for harsh criticism or, at the very least, tight-lipped silence.

"No problem." The bemused look on her face never wavered.

"Of course, it is," he countered. "I broke your fly rod."

"Yeah, but first rods always break." She took the pieces. The line remained intact, and she reeled it in. "That's why I wouldn't sell you that Sage you liked."

Sunlight glinted off the river and shimmered in Jess's hair. He stepped back, putting some distance between them so he wouldn't be as tempted to reach out and catch one of her curls in his fingers.

"I think I've done enough damage for one day," he suggested. They had an hour before his lesson ended, but standing close to her in such a secluded spot was too unnerving. And from the way Jess was looking at him, he thought she might be feeling the same thing. Still, he couldn't bring himself to leave just yet. A quick meal in neutral territory seemed like a good idea. "How about a bite to eat, instead?"

"Okay," she said after a moment, "but you're buying."

Watching the woman who opposed his plans slosh toward the shore, Dan wondered what he was getting himself into. But a smile still pulled at his lips as he followed her.

GIVEN THEIR CASUAL ATTIRE, the outdoor seating at Long Doggers made a good choice. While Dan headed for the walk-up window to place their order, Jess staked out seats at a picnic table. Sliding onto the wooden bench, she rubbed her arms to ward off a sudden chill that had nothing to do with the temperature that had risen right along with the sun. She was taking a chance by eating with the dangerously handsome man who had set his sights on Phelps Cove. Her plan to sway him over to her side of the development issue was too important—she couldn't allow herself to be distracted by the feelings he stirred within her. Determined not to let that happen, she drew on what she knew best and plotted her strategy while she laid out napkins and plastic cutlery. Didn't the one who understood the quarry always catch the most fish? So far, what she knew about Dan wouldn't help her win the battle. Sure, he could be full of himself, handing out orders he obviously expected to have obeyed, but there was more to him than that. She was sure of it. Like the foster care thing—she hadn't seen that coming. So, what other secrets did he have?

"Dan, what led you into medicine?" she asked once he had settled a numbered flag and their drinks on the table.

"It's what I've always wanted to do," he said, squeezing lemon into a glass of iced tea.

While he stirred and drank, she blew on her coffee to cool it and took a sip.

"And surgery?" She thought back to what he'd said in her office. "What made you choose thoracics?"

"Seems I have a talent for knife work," he said with a shrug that was both humble and endearing. "My mom's death steered me toward chest surgery."

The waitress appeared with their food just then, and

Jess tore into her egg burrito, using the interruption to think about her own family. Her parents had retired to the Carolina's before she married Tom but, even though she didn't see them often, the thought of losing them forever made her throat tighten. "How old were you when she passed?" she asked when they were alone again.

"Thirteen. Car accident. No seat belt." He bit into his breakfast sandwich as if it offended him.

Jess inhaled sharply. If anything happened to her, Adam had his grandparents and Sam to rely on, but parents were supposed to stick around for their children. That meant not racing across the shallows as much as it did showing up at PTA meetings and Little League. "There wasn't anyone who…?"

The way his jaw worked, Dan might have been chewing tough leather. He shook his head.

She blinked to clear a sudden dampness from her eyes. "Was it as bad as they say it is?" Horror stories about foster care made the news all too often.

He sipped his drink. "The system isn't easy, but I landed with people who kept me out of trouble. Took advantage of the free tuition at the state university. Grants, scholarships and loans got me through med school, so here I am."

"I didn't know college was part of the deal."

"There aren't many who get that far."

"Really?" It seemed unbelievable that someone with a free ride would chuck it all away. From the time she could recite her ABC's, her parents had let her know how important it was to get a good education. She intended to do the same for Adam.

"Kids in the system get moved around a lot." Jelly threatened to drip from the edges of his biscuit. Dan eased it onto the plate without losing a drop. "Especially if they have discipline problems. And without parents, who wouldn't? With all that shuffling, school records get lost. Kids are held back. Once discouraged, they quit school, take dead-end jobs and get locked into a life they wouldn't choose for themselves."

"You didn't," she pointed out before snagging a hash brown from his plate.

"I bounced around at first, but I wound up with a great set of foster parents. They preached the value of education. Made sure I talked the talk and walked the walk right through high school." His lips thinned and twisted to one side. "I still might not have made it, though, if they hadn't held on to me after I turned eighteen."

"What happened then?"

"It's called aging out," he said. "Medical care. Children and family services. Monthly stipend. They all stop. With no more support money, most caretakers turn the kids out onto the street. The result is an even higher drop-out rate. And that—" he stopped to sip his iced tea "—is why Connections House is so important."

"I'm not sure I follow," she said. She wasn't certain she wanted to, and pushed aside the remains of her burrito. At eighteen, she'd been a sophomore at Florida Tech. That summer, her biggest concern was how much spending money she'd earn working on the *Lucky Lady,* a deep-sea fishing charter out of Cape Canaveral. She couldn't imagine having had to survive on her own at that age.

"It's my answer to the problem." Dan grabbed a napkin and sketched as he talked. "It's a transitional housing complex where kids who age out of the system can live while they finish high school, prepare for college or learn the skills they need to get better jobs. I'm still in the planning stages, but when it's finished, counselors and mentors will teach everything from how to handle a checkbook to the importance of showing up to work on time. And there'll be an infirmary, since most of the kids won't have insurance."

She stared down at the rough outline of several cottages clustered around a larger, central building. His goal sounded like a worthy cause, an admirable one. One she'd give her whole-hearted support, as long as he built it anywhere but in Phelps Cove.

The solution seemed obvious enough. The customer base at On The Fly included practically every deep pocket in Brevard County. Surely, one of them owned land suited to Dan's project. She'd help him find the right spot, a move which would free them to...

To do what, exactly?

She shied away from an answer, choosing instead to concentrate on the beginnings of a plan. Her thoughts were interrupted when a well-dressed businessman stepped to the end of their table and cleared his throat. Immediately, Dan's relaxed manner vanished, replaced by the slightly arrogant demeanor that raised her hackles. Recognizing their visitor as an occasional customer in the shop, she nodded to him.

He swept the briefest of looks her way before turning his full attention to her client.

"Glad to run into you," he said. "I had planned to call this afternoon, but this saves the trouble. If you have a minute?"

"Of course, Bryce," Dan answered. He ran a napkin over his lips. "Let me settle our bill and I'll be right back." He rose, reaching for his wallet. "Jess, I'll see you next week?"

"Sure, I'll call your office with the details," she said to a retreating back. She gritted her teeth against the sting of a short dismissal and turned to the newcomer.

"You may not remember me, but I'm Jess Cofer," she said, managing a smile. "From On The Fly."

"Great store." Bryce's head bobbed. "You still carry those tube flies with five-ought hooks and poppers?"

Jess knew the ones. "We have 'em. Planning to hunt billfish, are you?" Big fish called for the expensive double-rigs.

"I'll need three dozen for a trip to Belize this spring," Bryce said. "Assorted colors. Keep them for me and I'll come by next month."

Only someone who never fretted over invoices would ask her to put several hundred dollars worth of stock on hold, but Bryce had given her another piece of the Dan Hamilton puzzle. Given what she already knew about his trip, it followed that the men were business partners, and who was she to resist an opportunity when it was handed to her?

"Dan was just telling me all about your charitable work with Connections House. It sounds like an amazing project, but I'm wondering if Phelps Cove is the ideal location. Something not so isolated might be better for young adults."

A flash of irritation crossed Bryce's face before his eyes narrowed into a calculating glare. "My only charitable work," he said, making the words sound like something he'd scrape from the bottom of his shoe, "is for the hospital. As for the land," he fumed, "its very seclusion makes it the ideal location for a surgical center catering to *my* exclusive clientele."

Jess folded her arms across her chest and leaned back

on the bench. Tom had always known just what to say to change her mind and, when it suited his purposes, he'd bent the truth. His lies had put her squarely behind the counter of On the Fly when all she'd wanted to do was start a guide service. Was Dan doing the same thing? Had he spun a story out of thin air to gain her sympathy? If so, the man was in for a rude awakening.

Her gaze shifted from the arrogant doctor at the end of the table to the one settling their tab. She'd put too much work into Phelps Cove to let anyone wreck the soon-to-be protected habitat.

"Excuse me," she said. "I'm needed back at the shop. As for the flies, they're first come, first served. If you want them, stop by and pick them up."

BRYCE WAS SCOWLING AT JESS'S DEPARTING TRUCK when Dan returned. "What on earth is your girlfriend's problem?" the plastic surgeon demanded.

Dan shook his head. "She's not my girlfriend."

The woman who adamantly opposed their plans for The Aegean could be fun-loving and, he suspected, fun to love, but he had sworn to keep his emotional distance.

Apparently not ready to let it go, Bryce blustered, "Good. She's not our kind of people. But why hang out with her if you two aren't seeing each other?"

"She's the guide I hired. She's improving my cast." In just a few short months, he'd have the skills he needed. That his technique was practically nonexistent? Well, that was something Bryce didn't need to know.

"Humph. She's a nervy one. You know she refused to set aside equipment I wanted to buy?"

Dan did his best not to look amused. Whatever the

reason, her reluctance gave him another chance to deepen his ties with The Aegean's leader.

"Not a problem, Bryce," he said. "I stop by On The Fly quite often. I'll grab whatever you want next time I'm in the store."

Looking suspiciously like the cat who'd swallowed the canary, Bryce smiled. "That's mighty nice of you." He swung another look toward the now-empty parking spot beside Dan's car. "You want to watch out for girls like that. She'd wind up taking you to the cleaners, the way Chase's wife is doing."

Slowly, Dan nodded. It was a timely reminder. Though marriage didn't factor into his immediate plans, he already knew the kind of woman he'd eventually wed. She'd be someone the elite of Brevard County's medical society could accept. Someone who organized hospital drives and fundraisers. Despite his growing respect for the woman who balanced motherhood with running a business and looked extremely attractive doing it, Jess could never be more than his fishing instructor. Or maybe a friend.

To distract them both, he switched topics. "I spoke with my financial manager. There's no problem meeting your schedule on the Merritt Island investment."

Bryce's demeanor changed in an instant. "Jack said you were the right man for our cadre." He gave Dan a wide smile. "Good to know you're on top of things."

"Always," Dan nodded.

It wasn't every day a man from his background was handed the two things he wanted most out of life— acceptance among his peers and the opportunity to fulfill his dream of helping today's foster kids make better lives for themselves. He couldn't afford to ruin his chance to achieve those goals. Another car swung into Jess's empty parking space and Dan turned away, determined that his future with the fly fisher would be strictly business.

Chapter Eight

Dan rotated the shapeless blob on the fly-tying vise. From his left hand, thread spooled over the tuft of fur in a perfectly smooth layer. He checked his progress against a color photograph and nodded. He might not be able to land a fish—yet—but surgery made him a whiz at tying knots. The finished product would fool even the most self-respecting bass into thinking it had found a nice juicy minnow. And wouldn't that surprise his instructor?

The spool in his hand slipped and he overlaid the thread, creating a bulge.

Darn it, Jess.

His plan to keep things strictly business with the cute guide wouldn't work very well if he continued to fantasize about kissing her. He stared down at a second mislaid thread. He had something to ask Jess and the longer he delayed it, the more his minnow was apt to resemble a lump of clay.

An hour later, the setting sun edged the horizon in red and gold as Dan climbed the stairs to Jess's apartment over the fly fishing shop. The door at the top of the stairs swung open so quickly when he knocked that for one brief moment, he let himself think she was anxious to see him. Of course, that idea only worked if she stood in the doorway. She didn't. Straight ahead, he saw nothing but light slanting through shutter slats on the other side of an immense loft. He looked down, straight into Adam's widening gaze.

The boy shouted over one shoulder. "Mom! Dr. Hamilton's here."

Quick footsteps sounded before a slim figure moved in front of the shutters. "Dan?"

She didn't sound all that happy to see him. He raised his head just as Jess stepped into a pool of lamplight. Irritation clouded her features and a chill he couldn't ignore filled her voice when she asked why he'd come.

"The shop was closed so I took a chance you'd be home. I need a favor."

Most people found it harder to turn him down in person, but not Jess. She held up a hand.

"Hold on a second."

Her focus dropped to the boy whose tiny face had scrunched into a curious look. Her voice sweetened. "Adam, could you play in your room?"

"But, Mom, I want to see Dr. Hamilton. He's my friend."

"Please go to your room." Jess's voice made it clear the request was nonnegotiable.

"Yes, ma'am," Adam said, but he didn't look happy about it. His little feet stomped down the hall.

Crossing her arms over her chest, Jess faced Dan again the minute a door slammed shut. "Let me make one thing clear. I've been burned by lies before and I won't tolerate being lied to again. If that's what you're all about, you'd better head right back down those stairs."

He could think of a dozen reasons why she wouldn't

want to see him. Phelps Cove was at the top of the list, but he was no liar.

"I haven't lied to you, Jess," he insisted. There were things he hadn't told her, but who didn't have a few secrets?

"Oh, yeah?"

He heard the challenge and squared his shoulders. Somewhere beneath her angry exterior was the intriguing woman he'd seen at Long Doggers. The more she dared him, the more determined he was to unearth her.

"What about your so-called home for foster kids? You said that was the reason you wanted to build in Phelps Cove. But Bryce didn't know anything about it."

"I never said we were *building it* there." He mentally gave himself a swift kick in the pants—he should never have left Bryce and Jess alone together. "That location is ideal for a cosmetic surgical center. My share of the profits from *that* venture will fund Connections House."

"Well, why didn't he say so?" Jess moved closer and her voice evened, but her rigid posture said she still wasn't convinced.

"Bryce doesn't share my interest in foster care." When she remained silent, he said softly, "I wouldn't lie to you, Jess. We don't share the same vision, but I'll be honest with you about it."

Though she uncrossed her arms, her stubborn attitude still showed in her posture.

"Huh," she huffed. "So, why are you here? I hope you have a good reason for showing up on my doorstep."

He did, though it took a second to remember that the boys and Regina were counting on him. At her invitation, he stepped into the main room of an apartment where a braided rug served as the roadway for a battalion of trucks and cars. Crayon drawings dominated artwork taped to the walls, reminding him that even a platonic relationship with Jess involved her son. He lingered near the door and got down to business.

"I need inexpensive fly rods for some kids I've been working with. Does On The Fly carry anything affordable?"

Confusion registered on Jess's face. "You're teaching?"

The way she asked, he couldn't tell whether she liked the idea or thought he was insane. Hoping for the former, he brushed a hand through his hair. "I wouldn't say that, exactly. I've been showing some of the foster kids what I've learned after dinner on Sundays."

"The cheapest rod we carry at On The Fly is still pricey. At— How many in your class?"

"I started out with Sean and Regina. Chris and Jose joined us this week. So, four."

"Four rods and reels. Fly line and backing," she whistled. "The bare necessities would run an easy two grand."

He shook his head. "That's a bit rich," he admitted. He'd hoped to get away with a couple of hundred dollars, not a couple of thousand.

"Now, hold on," Jess said when he mumbled his apologies and turned to leave. "I might have some equipment you can borrow. Let me sort through a few things and I'll bring whatever I have to your lesson on Wednesday."

As much as he wanted to take her up on the offer, she'd said first rods always broke, and he could prove it. Jess brushed his concerns aside.

"It's old gear, believe me. No need for anyone to have

a heart attack if something gets busted. Besides, it's just a loan until we figure out a permanent solution."

Liking the way she included him in the "we" equation more than he wanted to admit, he searched the room for a way to show his thanks—maybe there was something she needed. A glance at the rumpled blanket on the couch stirred an image of them both curled up beneath it, but he squelched the thought. Even if he wanted to steer their relationship in that direction, the pitter-patter of feet in the hallway reminded him that they weren't alone.

"Mom?" Adam said from the doorway. "I'm hungry."

Jess checked her watch. "Of course you are. Let's say goodbye to Dr. Hamilton and I'll fix some dinner."

Adam launched himself across the room and slammed into Jess's knees. His little arms wrapped around her thighs and he tipped his head up. "I want nuggets 'n' fries," the boy pleaded.

When Jess gave her head a rueful shake, Dan ruffled Adam's hair. He intended to commiserate with the child. Maybe say something about how all that salt and fat wasn't good for him anyway. He meant to say he'd see them around. Somehow, in the instant between telling himself he should go and actually saying goodbye, his words changed to, "Let me take you out to dinner."

"To McDonald's?" The boy was positively awestruck.

Adam's excitement made it impossible to suggest anyplace else. Not that it mattered. Jess had the final say, and if he was reading her right, her dinner plans didn't include an unexpected visitor.

"Hold on there, buddy," he said, despite a sudden

craving for fast food. "Let's wait to hear what your mom says."

Wishing he didn't care about the outcome, he held his breath and scoured Jess's face. Her gaze lifted from Adam to meet his, and a hesitant smile spread across her lips.

"Why not," she said.

WITH THE LAST OF THE STARS SPARKLING in a cloudless sky, Jess slipped behind the wheel of On The Fly's pickup truck. Light spilled from her living-room window, and she waved at the woman silhouetted there. Sam's wife Evy had arrived twenty minutes earlier. She'd see Adam off to school.

Jess threw the truck in gear. While she drove, she blew a warm breath over her fingers and breathed a prayer of thanks for good friends who kept her from having to drag her child through the cold to day care. Now, if only the other facets of her life would stabilize, she and Adam would be okay. But so far, they hadn't. And she couldn't shake the feeling that she'd let her guard down with Dan and would pay the consequences.

It had happened before with Tom.

She'd noted his rugged good looks the day they'd met, the same way she'd noticed his daredevil attitude, but he certainly hadn't hooked her at first glance. It was only after he'd sworn off driving too fast and diving too deep that she agreed to one date, and then another. They were married before she caught on to the fact that he'd simply redirected his risky behavior, investing all their savings in a business she never wanted. Once she discovered they were pregnant, he'd promised to settle down. And as far as she could tell, he had. Which made his death when she was eight months along with Adam an even bigger shock. One that sent her into early labor. After that, she'd tried to minimize the number of unexpected changes in her life.

Lately, though, she'd begun to feel as if she'd lost her grip again. Things were spinning out of control. On The Fly's bottom line continued to sink. Henry's death meant new challenges for Phelps Cove. As if that weren't enough, each day's newspaper carried another objection to the protected habitat. She hadn't foreseen any of it.

No more than she'd anticipated a growing attraction for the man who pulled to a stop beneath a billboard advertising one of the area's premier development projects. The man who'd treated her son to his favorite kid's meal and thus earned a place in the boy's heart. As Dan rounded his car and approached her truck, her own heart thudded unevenly. She hadn't thought there was a man alive who could make flannel look sexy, but Dan, with his broad chest and narrow waist, did just that. And his lithe form filled his jeans better than it had a right to do. Determined not to succumb to his charms, she took a deep breath and stepped from her vehicle.

"Glad you made it." Jess hated the way the cold—not Dan—made her voice tremble. "Brrr," she said, rubbing her hands together. "Ready to get your line wet?"

"Say what?" Dan's mouth hitched.

She grinned. "If you're going to be a fly fisher, you need to learn the lingo. Are you ready?"

His gaze swept beyond the edge of a small field to a housing development that spread in every direction. The edges of his smile drooped. "Where?"

"Right there." She pointed to a man-made pond within walking distance.

As if on cue, Dan lifted an eyebrow. The reaction was exactly what she'd expected, and she stifled a smile.

"Around here, wherever there's water, there are fish." She headed for the back of her truck and their equipment, stopping when he didn't follow.

Dan kicked a clod of dirt. "I don't know, Jess. I hear this area has some of the best fishing in the world. Your little pond doesn't look like it'll live up to that reputation."

"It's not one of my favorite fishing haunts." She crossed her arms and turned to face him. "But since you're paying me to teach you how to fly fish, I wanted a wide-open space where we could work on your technique." With nary a bush nor a tree in sight, the small lake offered plenty of room for Dan to practice his casts without having to worry about snagging a line or breaking a rod.

He squinted at the nearby houses. Row upon row of them were packed so closely together, one person could holler, "Pass the sugar," and have the neighbors on either side hand it in through an open window.

"Seriously?" he asked. "Have you taken a good look around here lately?"

Her chin firmed. "Yes, as a matter of fact, I have. And I'm just sick about it."

She hadn't planned on teaching another class on the environment this morning, but Dan's education had some serious holes, and she was just the person to fill them. She pulled herself erect.

"For more than a hundred years, cattle grazed this entire area." She spread her arms wide. "But with land prices on the rise, developers are building new homes wherever they can, and people are snapping them up.

What they fail to realize is that this land is basically a low-lying marsh."

Dan lifted one foot and examined his boot. Mud clung to the sole and climbed several inches up the sides. "The ground feels spongy," he admitted. "And it's wet."

"Yeah, and this is winter. The dry season. Wait till next summer when a hurricane dumps thirty or forty inches of rain in the area. People won't be so happy to live here, then."

He glanced up the road. "A few more retention ponds and better drainage ought to resolve any problems."

"You think? Do you know where that water goes?" She didn't pause long enough to let him answer. "It pours into ditches and drain pipes that lead straight into rivers. Which would be fine except for one thing. With so many people insisting on green, weed-free lawns, the runoff is loaded with nitrates and fertilizers. That stuff is lethal," she said heatedly. "We used to give nature a chance by letting the ground filter out some of the toxins. Not anymore. Now, instead of maintaining natural barriers—like the land around Phelps Cove—we build right up to the waterline."

She'd said too much and almost felt sorry for Dan when he threw up his hands in a gesture that was as much a plea for her to stop as it was his signal that he'd had enough.

"Okay, Jess. You've made your point. Development is bad for the environment. I get it."

While he stomped his feet to shake the mud from his boots, she forced herself to take a cleansing breath. Somehow, it didn't feel nearly as good as she thought it should to be on the right side of an argument when he was her opponent.

Dan aimed a thumb toward the residential streets.

"You might want to think about where these people are going to live if we don't build houses for them. Last time we talked, you said things were slow at On The Fly, right?"

"Yeah, I guess." It wasn't something she was proud of, but she couldn't very well lie about it. Not when she insisted on the truth from everyone else.

"Believe me, Jess, the sagging economy affects everyone. Growth is one of the answers. And growth means bringing in more new businesses, and the people to run them. And that means building houses." He paused before adding, "And medical facilities."

"Yeah, like everyone *needs* a facelift," she muttered. But she couldn't ignore the kernel of truth in his words. Eyes narrowing, she stared at him while she pondered his point, thinking of the counterarguments she could use. He must have been one step ahead of her, though, and sent the conversation in a different direction.

"I think we've spent enough time on this for one morning. For now, why don't we just agree to disagree?" Reaching around to his back, he pulled a folded newspaper from his waistband. "Besides, I have something else I wanted to show you."

Jess eyed the paper warily. The morning edition had carried another letter complaining about the state's plans for Phelps Cove. She wasn't in the mood to hear Dan gloat over it any more than she wanted to continue arguing about his misguided plans for property she considered a sacred trust.

"You going to catch up on your reading while you're out here?" she asked hopefully.

"Cute." His smile widened. "I found an ad for fly rods I thought you should see. Cheap ones. The two you lent me are great, but I want the kids to have their own equipment. You think these would be all right?"

Bright red ink drew her attention to the Sporting Goods column. She studied the ad he'd circled. It touted an unbelievably low price, and recognizing the phone number of a competitor, she knew why.

"This ad isn't for fly rods. He's selling rod-building kits. Tons of assembly required," she noted. "I'm guessing that's not what you had in mind."

"Not hardly. Glad I ran it by you before I gave him a call."

Jess saw Dan's shoulders sag a little and knew he was more disappointed than he wanted to let on. "Don't worry," she said, feeling more at ease now that they'd put their disagreement aside. "I'm pretty sure I know where we can get what you need. Are you up for a road trip on Saturday?"

Dan's head lifted and a smile lit his face. "I'm tied up till midmorning, but anytime after that is fine. Where are we headed?"

She put a finger to her lips. "Can't tell," she grinned. Turning to lower the truck's tailgate, she added, "We should probably get started before noon. You can pick us up at the shop. Adam and me. You don't mind if I bring him, do you?"

"Great idea. It'll be good to see him again."

The speed at which Dan welcomed a trip with her— and her son—nearly took her breath away. More than that, the warm glow it ignited in the pit of her stomach rocked her back on her heels. Jess hadn't realized how much she wanted him to approve her plans. She grabbed a pair of lightweight fly rods from the back of the truck and thrust one into his outstretched hand. "We use a different weight rod for freshwater," she explained before gesturing for him to lead the way to the pond.

While she trailed behind him, Jess mulled over all the things she'd learned about the successful doctor. He'd seen the results of risky behavior and chosen a different path for himself. He spent his spare time helping kids and young adults. And he was certainly easy on the eyes. In short, he met all the criteria she'd listed for Sam the day he'd broached the subject of her nonexistent love life. As she tried to ignore the woodsy scent that drifted in Dan's wake, she had to admit that the guy was darn near perfect.

If, that was, she overlooked his stance on Phelps Cove. A horrifying thought that, she reminded herself, was a deal breaker.

Joining Dan at the water's edge, she was careful to keep her distance from the novice fly fisher. Moments later, he shot a cast into the middle of the pond.

"Hey, that's not fair," Jess complained. She added a smile just to let him know she was teasing. "You've been practicing."

"Maybe a little bit." Dan nodded. He retrieved enough line to make another cast.

"When?" Knowing his tight schedule, she was amazed that he'd found the time.

"Lunch hours," he said as the business end of his line landed dead-center in the water. "My office building overlooks the river."

"You keep that up and I'll be able to take you out in the boat sooner than I planned." If he was headed to Belize, he'd need to master the art of casting from a deck that rocked on ocean swells.

Her own rod nestled in the crook of one arm, she congratulated herself on taking only the occasional peek at the way Dan's neck muscles bunched when he drew the rod back, or the way they eased when he whipped it forward. His technique had improved more than she'd anticipated and, satisfied that he had the basic cast down pat, she moved on to the next lesson.

"Okay, let's see you strip."

The words were barely out of her mouth when Dan tugged at his shirt collar.

"If you insist," he said with an impudent grin.

"Lingo, Hamilton, lingo," she reminded, though her overheated cheeks probably ruined the stern look. She cast into the water. With gentle tugs, she "stripped," making the lure swim in short, fish-attracting spurts while excess fly line spiraled into a neat pile at her feet.

"You got it?" She glanced at Dan to make sure he'd followed and caught him watching her with a bemused expression she knew had nothing to do with fly fishing.

Suddenly anxious to change the topic, she pointed to a young alligator lazing in the winter sun on the opposite side of the man-made lake. "That fella keeps the population down, so anything you catch will have a small mouth. A gentle tug is all it takes to set the hook when you get a bite."

Five minutes later, he did. While she offered encouragement, Dan smoothly followed her instructions until a six-inch bream splashed in the shallow water at his feet. His face broke into a huge smile.

"Congratulations," Jess called. "Your first catch on a fly line."

"My first catch, period," Dan reminded her.

She whipped a digital camera from her vest pocket.

"We need to snap this big guy's picture and get him back in the water."

Everything about Jess went soft as she peered through the viewfinder at the tall man who wore a goofy grin while he held up the tiny fish. In the second before she snapped his picture, she wondered how a boy who'd been denied so much had overcome such awful circumstances. He'd not only stayed in school, he'd excelled. And now he was giving back, working to help other kids create better lives for themselves.

"So…" Her throat had grown tight and she didn't trust her voice. Silently, she demonstrated how to slide the hook from the fish's mouth while pretending she didn't see the questioning glances from the man at her elbow. She released his catch into the water before she turned to face him. "So," she tried again. "Tell me the story. Why didn't you fish as a kid?"

"It's not all that special." He shrugged. "I almost went…once."

When he didn't volunteer more, she ordered, "Out with it, Hamilton."

"Okay, but only because you asked so nicely." Dan smiled and tugged his sunglasses off his face. "I'd been with this one family a couple of months when they started making plans for summer vacation. We were all going to Tennessee, they said, to do a little fishing. We spent weekends scrounging around yard sales for rods and reels. Even visited a bait shop where I spent my chore money on the shiniest lure I could find." He shook his head, reminiscing. "I'd nearly forgotten that lure. It was bright red with black slashes painted on the sides to resemble fins. It rattled when I shook it."

"A crank bait," she offered.

Dan's eyes lit up. "Yeah, that's what the man at the

bait shop called it. The crazy thing had enough hooks hanging off it, I knew I'd catch a monster of a fish."

"Maybe," she nodded, though snagging one of the sharp treble hooks on a log was more likely. She kept the observation to herself. "So what happened?"

"The day before we were supposed to leave, a social worker showed up saying she'd found an even better placement. She had me packed up and moved out of the house so fast, I left the lure behind." Dan stared at the horizon. "I always wondered if anybody caught a fish with it." He shrugged. "Years later, I found out there was a rule against taking foster kids out of state."

Jess wiped the corner of one eye and wasn't a bit surprised when her fingers came away damp. "I can't imagine…" Her voice died.

"It worked out," he said, focusing on her once more. "Turned out, she was right about the new family. I still have dinner with Glen and Maddy most Sunday afternoons." He smiled softly. "You should come with me sometime," he said. "Bring Adam. Does he like basketball?"

"He's a boy. Anything that involves running around and making noise is right up his alley."

"He'd like these guys, then. They love sports. So, you'll come?"

Jess knew one of them was going to lose the battle over Phelps Cove and the smartest thing she could do was to walk away. But when Dan's brown eyes searched hers for an answer, she let her heart do the talking. "Sure," she whispered. "I'd like that."

He edged forward until all she could see was the soft gray plaid covering his chest. The space between them filled with his unique woodsy scent. A hunger to taste him flared, and she swiped her tongue past her lips.

When she tipped her head back, his eyes drew her into their depths. Reason sent up one final warning flare that fizzled. She inhaled another breath and her being filled with Dan's presence.

Slowly, ever so slowly, he lowered his lips to hers. She knew he was giving her ample opportunity to back away. As much as she appreciated it, now that she'd committed to the kiss, she had no intention of going anywhere. She meant to stand her ground, but her feet betrayed her and shifted forward, letting him know she couldn't wait another second.

As she rose on tiptoe to meet him, his lips grazed hers and she gasped, closing her eyes and relishing sensations she'd locked away for too long. His tongue teased her lips with warm touches until she opened to let him in. Warmth turned to white heat. His mouth fused to hers. Their tongues danced, each move sending tiny flames of desire arcing to her core.

His hand found her waist and drew her ever closer. Pressed against him, she wanted more and ran one palm over the bunched muscles of his shoulders to thread her fingers through his hair. She longed to follow the curve of his ribs and skim her hand along the narrowness of his waist.

But she couldn't. Not unless she let the fly rod she was still holding clatter to the ground. She slanted one eye open, hoping for a soft spot to let it fall. One glimpse of navy graphite was all it took to ruin the moment. She stared, realizing the rod she'd grabbed was one of Tom's old favorites. With a half gasp, she stepped out of Dan's arms.

Dan backed away. "I didn't mean—" he began.

"It's all right," she rushed to assure him. "I just... I just need to take things slow." Slower than her heart, which was belting out a jazz beat against her rib cage. "That okay with you?"

"Look, Jess, I don't want to push it. We're attracted to each other. That may be all it is. Not that that's a bad thing," he said with an understanding grin that lightened the mood and put her at ease. "But if there's something more, we have time to figure it out."

"Okay, then." She backed away. Thinking was not an option with six-plus-feet of Dan Hamilton anywhere in the vicinity. "I'll see you Saturday," she said, intending to use the intervening time to clear her head.

Chapter Nine

Sunshine, blue skies and the better part of a day off—
what else could a man ask for?

Not a whole lot. Dan grinned as he pulled to a stop at
the foot of a wooden staircase that ran along the backside of On The Fly. Thanks to a few referrals from his
new business associates, his already-thriving practice
was doing even better. Word around the poker table at
Bryce's last week had assured him that plans for the
surgical center were moving forward. And though he'd
initially seen the sport only as a means to impress his
partners, he'd even developed a fondness for fly fishing.
Not that he could overlook the way some aspects of the
hobby complicated matters.

Thirty days ago, having a child hadn't been a priority.
But now, looking at the little boy who practically flew
down the steps from Jess's apartment, he had to wonder
why.

"Hi, Dr. Hamilton. Mom says we're going on a scav-
enger hunt. That's like a treasure hunt."

One glimpse of the ear-to-ear grin Adam wore with
his T-shirt and basketball shorts poked a hole in Dan's
stoic facade just above his heart. The kid was too fast
for him, jerking open the Beamer's passenger door and

bouncing into the car almost before he had a chance to shift into Park. A machine-gun volley of words rose from the backseat.

"Do you like treasure hunts? I do. Do you think we'll see pirates? I asked Mom and she said no, but don't you think we'll see a pirate if we hunt for buried treasure?"

"Whoa, tiger. That's a lot of questions all at once," he interrupted. "Let's wait and see what your mom has to say."

Jess, the source of his conflicting emotions, sped down the stairs nearly as quickly as her child. Watching the way her curls sparkled in the midmorning sun, he gave his head a rueful shake. He'd done some serious thinking after their last fishing lesson and the kiss that still kept him awake nights. Jess wasn't the polished, sophisticated woman his business associates would approve of, but his heart argued that she was exactly the kind of woman *he* wanted.

Unfortunately, their opposing interests in Phelps Cove made a romantic relationship impossible. He felt a pang of regret for what might have been as she reached into her pickup truck for Adam's booster seat. Once Dan completed his fishing lessons, he and Jess would go their separate ways. Hopefully, not as bitter enemies, although his involvement with The Aegean might lead to that. In the meantime, or until his business partners finalized their purchase of the land she treated as her own, couldn't they at least be friends?

And friends helped one another, didn't they?

While Adam mashed buttons on his armrest, Dan slipped from behind the wheel.

"Here, let me get that for you." He leaned in, brushing his lips across Jess's cheek in the kind of greeting one friend would give another. Light danced in her dark eyes. She smelled of orange blossoms…

Behind him, the Beamer's back window glided down.

"C'mon, Mom," Adam called. "C'mon, Dr. Hamilton. Let's go."

Dan stepped back quickly. Trying to convince his heart to listen to his mind, he took the car seat from Jess and followed her instructions for installing it.

"Let's go see the pirates," Adam commanded before he was finished.

"No pirates," Jess said to the boy's obvious displeasure. Squatting, she settled a hand on his knee. "But we might see some animals. If you behave yourself, you'll get to pet them."

Adam peered up through dark eyes that were very much like his mother's. "I like dogs, not cats." His small face lifted. "I know lots of knock-knock jokes. Do you, Dr. Hamilton?"

"I did once upon a time," Dan admitted. Two, maybe three decades had passed since he told his last one.

Adam grinned. "Okay, you first."

There was a trick in there somewhere, but it had been too long to remember. Dan glanced at Jess for help, but she shrugged, smiling, and stepped away from the car. He was on his own. "Knock, knock," he said slowly.

"Who's there?" The child didn't wait for an answer but started laughing immediately.

"You got me." He messed with Adam's hair and laughed along with the boy.

"Get it?" Adam piped. "I said, 'You start,' and you didn't know what to say."

"Yep. Now, hold on a sec. Let me get directions from your mom, or we'll never get where we're going.

"Where are we headed?" Dan turned to Jess without having to pretend he was enjoying himself. He hadn't had a chance to really look at her, but with an antsy Adam calling the shots, he settled for a quick study of the soft white T-shirt she wore over snug jeans. His perusal dropped to tanned and shapely ankles. In deference to the warm weather, Jess wore flip-flops, her pink toenails glistening.

"Yeah, Mom. Where are we going? How long will it take? Will we be there soon?" Adam asked.

"It's still a secret." Jess gave them a mischievous smile before settling into the Beamer's passenger seat.

Content to have her company and Adam's wherever they were headed, Dan followed piecemeal directions across the causeway, through quaint Cocoa Village and northbound onto I-95. While Florida's never-ending flatness streamed past the car, he and Jess swapped stories about work and life. Meanwhile, Adam pulled action characters from a bag and filled the holes in their conversation with the noise of swooping bat wings and knockout punches. Jess was in the middle of a story about one of her biology professors when the child interrupted.

"Mom, next time we go fishing, I wanna use worms."

A silence so profound descended on the car that Dan risked a glance away from his intense study of the road ahead. He was just in time to catch the look of disgust Jess quickly masked before she swung to face her son.

"Fly fishers never use bait," she said the way someone might quote from a rule book.

"Well, Tommy D. said his dad took him fishing and they used worms and it was neat. I want to fish with worms, too." More swooping noises ensued as Adam returned to his game.

Jess faced forward and moaned into her hands. "Not even six years old, and he's ruined. What kind of fly fishing guide lets her son use bait? I won't be able to walk down Main Street unless I put a bag over my head." She clutched her heart. "What will Sam say?"

"Maybe it's just a phase," Dan offered. Fly fishers were a strange bunch. They'd sooner toss a bait fisher overboard than let him contaminate their boat. "Adam, didn't I hear you turned up your nose at chicken nuggets last week?"

"Yep," the boy quipped proudly. "I like sandwiches now. Tommy D. says chicken nuggets are for babies."

Dan suppressed a growl. "Who is this Tommy D. kid?"

"Best friend," Jess whispered. "Don't get too wrapped up in what he says. Kids this age change their minds twice a week. Not that I wouldn't mind the occasional burger now and then." She sighed. Pointing, she directed, "Turn off at the next exit."

A bad feeling rumbled through him when he read the familiar highway sign. With every turn, hope that he'd guessed wrong about their ultimate destination faded, and his stomach sank lower. It was practically rolling around on the floorboards by the time he drove onto the dirt-and-grass lot and parked beneath the sign for the Daytona Beach Flea Market.

"Surprised?" The expectant look of a kid walking into a candy store with five bucks in her pocket glowed on Jess's face. Adam had already unsnapped his seat belt and was bouncing on his booster chair.

Dan didn't share their excitement, and he had the churning stomach to prove it. "That's one way to put it. Why are we here?"

"To get you the rods for your class, of course," she

answered as if he should already possess that bit of information.

The woman who owned a fly shop had brought him here? "I can afford better," he protested.

"I know, but c'mon. It'll be fun. You'll see." She was halfway out the door, but stopped to swivel a questioning look over her shoulder. "Haven't you been to a flea market before?"

"Far too often," he said through clenched teeth. He'd been to this particular one so often he could name the rows of tin-covered booths where women with big hair and chaw-chewing men sold factory thirds and fourths, clothes that wouldn't last through the first wash and dry. He'd left his days of shopping at big-box stores and the Daytona freaking flea market behind long ago, along with all the other anxieties that came with being a ward of the state.

Jess's eyes turned thoughtful. "There's a guy here, sells fly rods cheap. If you have a better solution to your equipment problem, I'm listening." She spared a look at Adam. "Besides, I promised him we'd stop at the petting zoo."

When she put it that way, he didn't have much choice. Acting like a spoiled child in front of Adam was not part of his image. And if he was going to come through for Sean and Regina, to say nothing of Chris and Jose and whoever else joined their merry little band next week, he had to grit his teeth and go along with the plan. He opened his car door, wincing at the unforgettable smell of overripe fruit.

So much for any hope that things had changed in the twenty years since his last visit.

He squared his shoulders and pulled down his game face while Jess took the lead. Holding tightly to Adam's hand, she disappeared behind a curtain of long plastic strips designed to keep flies and bugs outside the cooler, darker produce section. He matched her steps, and with Adam between them, they moved down clothing aisles crowded with too many familiar-looking families. Kids clustered around tables where a dollar bought a pair of jeans with blown-out knees. There wasn't enough soap in the world to purge the smell of someone else's sweat from shirts that sold for fifty cents.

He shuddered and kept his feet moving, his emotions under tight control until she led them down a side aisle he'd never seen before. Once they were out of the main traffic flow, his tension eased and, in short order, they walked into a jumbled mess of a tackle store housed in an enormous wooden crate. Adam ran ahead to the sales counter where lures and barbed hooks overflowed from large plastic tubs perched on rickety folding tables. He started sorting through them, barely looking up when Jess gestured to car-size fans on either side of the entry.

"They're for air boats," she explained in answer to Dan's questioning gaze.

"Adam," she called, "you can look around, but don't go past the blowers."

"Okay," he answered as he busily sorted lures by color.

She gestured toward fishing poles that sprouted from an old rain barrel and suggested Dan take a look. Several fly rods stood among them. Once they'd selected a few, she reached for the one he liked best and placed her smaller hands on his.

"Feel the bounce?" she asked. "Choosing a rod is all about personal preference. Is it as limber or as stiff as you'd like?"

He chuckled low in his chest. "It'll do," he said with a knowing smile and watched her cheeks warm.

The teasing grin she shot him as she fanned her face nearly made him laugh out loud. Not wanting to explain the joke to their three-foot chaperone, he stifled the urge.

Jess nodded toward the rods he'd set aside. "How about a couple more? They don't cost much, and buying them now will save you a trip back."

"Doesn't sound like my teacher has faith in my ability to teach. What does that say about her?"

"It says she understands the sport. Now go on." She pushed him lightly. "Two more, and we'll check out. Next stop, the petting zoo. Then, you can treat Adam and me to supper."

His pulse had ramped up when Jess's hand lingered on his chest longer than necessary, but the frown that slipped over his face was as unintended as he was powerless to stop it.

"Here?" he asked. The idea of eating at the food court didn't work for him.

"I had my heart set on a funnel cake," she answered, looking sheepish.

"For you, anything." With a gentle hand, he lifted her chin until her eyes met his. "But after that, how about a restaurant? I know several near here."

She brightened. "Might as well take advantage of Adam's new and improved menu choices."

Dan turned to Adam. "Hey, kiddo, you still hankering to see those pirates?"

The servers at Peg Leg's dressed in pantaloons and tricorn hats. Captain Kidd adorned the menu. Adam would love it, and casting a look between Jess and her son, Dan had the feeling he would, too.

"WHAT DO YOU SAY TO DR. HAMILTON, Adam?" Jess asked at the end of a day her son had enjoyed as much as she had. When Adam didn't answer, she swung a look into the backseat. The streetlamps around On The Fly bathed the child in bluish light.

Adam slumped against the car door. His mouth gaped open, and his limbs had gone loose and liquid—he was sound asleep. The tricorn hat Dan had made from the kiddie menu at dinner listed precariously to one side.

"He's out," she whispered. When had that happened? She'd have sworn he was still cracking one-liners as they crossed the causeway and made the final turn for home.

"'Bout time he wound down." Dan grinned. "I thought he was going to outlast me."

"You were good with him," she said with a grateful smile. Not many men could deal with an active five-year-old, but Dan was a natural. The two guys had talked virtually nonstop from the minute a one-eyed pirate had guided them to their seats in "the galley" of Peg Leg's, until an appropriately garbed "serving wench" slid burgers and fries onto the table. The hungry boy had stopped eating only long enough to listen, wide-eyed, as the staff gathered around a nearby table and yo-ho-ho'd their way through the restaurant's version of the birthday song.

Dan shifted to face her. "He's an easy kid to be around. I had fun." He leaned forward and batted the red-and-black lure that hung from the rearview mirror. "Thanks for that," he said with a soft smile.

Jess swore she'd seen tears shimmer in the man's eyes when Adam had given him their gift in the pause between dinner and dessert. "You ever think of having a child of your own?" she asked. "You'd make a good dad." It didn't take an empath to recognize Dan's aversion to flea markets, but whatever demons the man fought, he'd overcome them to make the day enjoyable for Adam's sake, as well as hers.

"I like to take things in order. Love and marriage are still pretty far down on my To Do list."

"I hear ya." she nodded. It wasn't easy, being both mom and dad to her little guy. Mostly, they made it work, but nights like tonight were tough. Especially when seeing Dan and her son together reminded her of all the things her little boy was missing out on by not having his own father around.

She hoped Adam wouldn't get attached to Dan too quickly. "Be careful, or you'll replace Tommy D. as Adam's best friend," she warned, trying to keep things light.

"Never happen," Dan said firmly. "I have it on good authority—" he nodded toward the sleeping figure in the backseat "—that Tommy D. walks on water." His seat belt retracted with a snap. "I'll carry Adam upstairs for you."

"Sure." She exhaled the word on a long, low breath. She'd agonized over how to invite Dan in for coffee without coming across as too forward—to say she was out of practice was an understatement.

Upstairs, she plucked the hat from her son's head and set it on his dresser where he'd see it first thing in the morning. Dan had stepped into the bathroom by the time Adam was all tucked in. With coffee next on the agenda, she headed for the kitchen.

In the light of the half-moon shining through the window, she fumbled with the pot.

Coffee. That's all it was. Coffee.

She wasn't going to bed with Dan, the man who

threatened all she stood for. And certainly not while Adam slept in the next room. But watching the handsome doctor with her son had stirred too many thoughts of how things might have been if Tom had lived. And that left her feeling unsettled, adrift.

She had loved her husband. A part of her always would. Sam, Evy, her parents—they all thought she'd kept other men at arm's length out of loyalty. She was the only one who knew it was the way Tom had lied to her that'd left her angry and afraid to trust.

Dan's honesty set him apart. It was one of the reasons that, despite frequent reminders not to fall for the doctor, she was drawn to him. Yes, the man had the sexy good looks that could turn a girl on with a single glance, but she was attracted to him on a much deeper level. By the time she finished pouring water into the coffeemaker, she was wondering if she shouldn't make one more effort to convince him to see things her way.

Soft footsteps in the hallway alerted her to Dan's presence moments before the comfortable weight of his hand settled on her shoulder.

"Do you mind?" he whispered in her ear.

Was he kidding? How could she object when the simple touch of his fingers shot tremors straight to her core and dampened her palms? He sifted through her hair, lifting and separating the strands. She rested her shoulders against his broad chest and concentrated on breathing until her heart beat in sync with his.

"Dan, I..." She turned to face him.

"It's okay," he said, sliding velvet hands along both sides of her jaw. "We won't take this any further than you want to go."

"Yeah, about that." Her breath hitched. She finished in a rush. "We need to talk."

Dan leaned away from her. His lips curved into a teasing smile. "Talk? Not coffee and whatever?"

"I'm serious. We need to hash this out before things go any further between us."

The crease between Dan's brows deepened. "What are you trying to tell me?"

She'd never been one to pussyfoot around the truth. "I'm saying I'd like to get to know you better." She threw in a flirty smile. "A lot better." She paused to let the meaning sink in before she added, "But…"

"Here it comes."

Nodding, she took a breath. "But I've never told you how my husband died, have I?"

Dan's look turned solemn. He leaned back, propping long arms against the kitchen island. "A boating accident. That's all I know."

She blew out some air. Drew in some more to steady herself, and began.

"Tom enjoyed spending time with our customers a whole lot more than he liked fishing. But once I was pregnant with Adam he took over the guide service. His clients that day were from New York. A couple of surgeons, actually." She nodded when Dan winced. They both understood the parallel. "From what they said later, they were in a hurry to get their lines wet. They were on their way to the point off Phelps Cove and dared Tom to take a shortcut on the north side of the Barge Canal."

Her words slowed. The facts were out there. The media'd had a field day, revealing every heartbreaking detail, but she'd sidestepped all the interviews and, ever since, she'd avoided discussing the accident with anyone. Until now. If she had any hope of changing Dan's mind about the cove, he needed to hear the whole story.

"The thing is, I'd taken those clients out before and

knew they were trouble. Tom and I had agreed not to guide them again. At least, I thought we had. When I found out he'd lied to me about who he was taking out that day, we fought. It was the last time I saw him alive."

Dan shifted forward. As much as she wanted to bury herself in his arms, she waved him off.

"Tom loved living on the edge, and that wasn't the first time I'd caught him in a lie."

She cleared her throat. After all this time, the disloyal words still nearly choked her.

"He ran the boat aground at top speed. The clients were okay except for a couple of scrapes and bruises, but Tom was thrown. Broke his neck. They airlifted him to the Trauma Center. There, uh…" She toed a spot on the linoleum. "There was no hope. Two days later, on my way home from the funeral, I went into early labor with Adam and nearly lost him, too."

She hugged herself. "And that's why I worked with Henry to preserve Phelps Cove."

"You see the land as a memorial to Tom." Compassion glinted in Dan's dark eyes.

Slowly, she nodded. "For a long time, I did. But it's really more for Adam." She swung her arms wide. "Preserving the cove is something we need to do for our future. I want to take my son fishing there. I want my grandkids to collect oyster shells and see horseshoe crabs crawl through the shallows. I want their kids to grow up knowing that panthers and turtles aren't just animals in a zoo." She swallowed a few tears.

"We've known from the day we met that we'd never see eye-to-eye about the land, Jess. I wish things were different, but there it is."

She glanced up at the kind, but clearly misguided man

who was dangerously close to stealing her heart. Reeling herself in, she kicked her foot against the floor.

"The legislature *is* going to purchase Phelps Cove. When they do, you'll lose your only way to make the money you need for Connections House. I'm just saying—The Aegean's surgery center could go practically anywhere. For not much more than the cost of clearing the land, you could demolish and rebuild wherever you wanted."

The look on Dan's face told her she'd given him something to think about. And when he nodded slowly, more to himself than to her, she felt a flicker of hope that things might work out between them.

"You make a good case," Dan said at length. "I think Bryce has already considered all the options, but I can certainly mention the idea of finding a different spot." He held up a hand. "No promises, though."

Whether it would be enough to persuade The Aegean group to give up their bid or not, well, for that, she'd just have to wait and see. As for any hope of a relationship with Dan, if it was going to work between them, there were things about her he'd need to accept. She tended to get passionate about what she believed in, and Phelps Cove wasn't the only thing that generated strong feelings.

She tilted her face to his. Her eyes locked on the contours of his lips, she watched as, ever so slowly, he leaned toward her. The tender kisses he planted on either side of her mouth stirred a hunger to have his lips on hers. She rose on tiptoe to meet him. The first brush of his lips was warm and inviting and, feeling as if she'd finally come home after being away too long, she sank against him.

The tip of his tongue sent little shock waves pulsing

through her, and she opened to welcome him. She smiled against his kisses. He tasted of mint with the smallest hint of chocolate syrup from the sundae they'd shared at dinner. As their tongues danced, she twined her hands through his hair. Thick and silky, it slipped through her fingers like satin and filled the air with the clean, crisp scent of falling rain.

Each kiss made her greedy for more. A look into Dan's heated gaze told her he was feeling the same thing. His hands eased to her waist and, with less effort than she imagined, he lifted her onto the counter. Her breasts swelled and grew impossibly heavy when he kissed the bare skin above her neckline. On fire with the need to feel his skin beneath her hands, she tugged his shirttail free of his jeans. She sighed softly when she brushed her fingers across the firm yet supple muscles of his chest.

Her breath ratcheted up with each caress, and she sucked in a gasp when his hand cupped her through the lacy fabric of her bra. She moved her hands around to his back, drawing him to her while his lips nibbled lower. Her heart pounded against her chest until she tingled all over. An incredible sweetness pooled below her waist when he fanned a breath across each breast.

It wasn't enough. It wasn't nearly enough. Pretty sure the anticipation was going to drive her mad, she scootched forward a notch.

A loud cry erupted from Adam's room, and they both jumped.

Jess knew she would have fallen off the edge of the counter if Dan's strong arms hadn't been there to catch her. Of course, she wouldn't have been on the counter if Dan hadn't been standing there, doing all those incredible things with his hands, his fingers, his tongue....

Her breath escaped in a ragged sigh when another wail came from the back of the apartment.

"Nightmare," she gasped. "He gets them. I need to…"

"Of course. Sure." Dan was already backing away, slipping buttons into holes and breathing almost as hard as she was. She jerked her T-shirt into place seconds before Adam stumbled to a halt outside the kitchen.

"Mom?"

"Yeah, baby." Jess slid off the kitchen counter and eased around Dan. "I'm right here, honey. Did you wake up?"

His favorite teddy bear clutched to his chest, Adam stood in the doorway. Tear-stained cheeks and hiccups told her the dream had been a bad one. She dropped to her knees, gathering him in her arms. Amazed at how fragile her sturdy little boy became in the middle of the night, she rocked him gently while she stroked his hair until he quieted.

"Want Mommy to warm some milk for you before you go back to bed?"

It was part of their routine and, his head pressed against her shoulder, Adam nodded.

"Climb up into your chair and I'll get it ready for you."

Two brown eyes widened as Adam stepped away from her and got his first good look at the other person in the kitchen.

"Did you have a bad dream, too?" He turned to Jess. "Mom, are you fixing him some?"

She bit back a nervous giggle and quirked a half smile at the light that danced in Dan's eyes.

"Warm milk sounds like just what the doctor ordered," Dan said, sliding into a chair opposite her son. "And I'm a doctor, so I should know."

A few seconds in the microwave took the chill off. Soon Adam's soft slurps punctuated the companionable silence that filled the kitchen. Jess eyed the boy who was rapidly growing sleepy again.

"Ready for bed?" she asked.

Adam nodded and slid from his chair before aiming an accusatory look at Dan. "You didn't drink it. Mom says we have to."

"Will do," Dan agreed softly. He wrapped long fingers around his own cup and downed a swig just as Adam peered up at him and asked, "Are we having a sleepover?" A huge yawn escaped his milk-rimmed lips. "Mom makes waffles when my friends sleep over. You'll like 'em."

"Maybe some other time," Dan answered with a deep chuckle that filled the quiet kitchen.

Mortified, Jess hurried to point out that the man across the table had his own home, with his own bed to sleep in before she hurried her child off to his room. By the time she exited Adam's room after another round of prayers and hugs had eased the boy back to sleep, Dan stood at the front door, one hand on the knob.

"We probably shouldn't press our luck. He might wake up again."

She wanted to argue, but she was already nodding. She might want to finish what they'd started in the kitchen, but permanence wasn't in the hand they'd been dealt, and shielding Adam from the day when their differences drove them apart was her responsibility. She brushed a final kiss on the soft underside of his chin. Inhaling his spicy scent one more time, she turned aside so he wouldn't see the sparkle of tears in her eyes.

"See you Wednesday," she whispered as she listened to him descend the stairs.

Edgy, restless and afraid he'd made off with a chunk of her heart when he left, Jess closed the door and leaned against it. Her glance slid across cedar floors, worn carpets and chintz curtains. For the seven years since she and Tom had opened On The Fly, the roomy apartment had been her home. Adam had never lived anyplace else. Not everyone had it so lucky, and Dan was one of those.

What had it been like for him, growing up without a place to call his own? Never knowing, when he headed off to school in the morning, if he'd sleep in the same bed that night? How had he coped? Especially after he'd aged out of the system, when—without Glen and Maddy's support—only his own determination, intelligence and drive would have stood between him and a life on the streets.

Small wonder that Connections House was so important to him.

He was sure to hold it against her when the fulfillment of her dream cost him his. But did it *have* to be that way? Right now, she and Dan were in a lose-lose situation with no hope of a relationship, but maybe—just maybe—she knew a way to fix things.

The possibility gave her plenty to think about during the long, sleepless night that followed.

Chapter Ten

His line swished through the crisp winter air. With a flick of the wrist, Dan landed the curve cast exactly where he wanted it—three feet off the bow of a rotting sailboat that had sunk during the last hurricane. Jess said they were sure to find a few snook hanging out around the structure. Seconds later, her fly landed a respectful ten yards away.

"Nice," she called. "But you didn't learn that cast from me. Where'd you pick it up?"

He followed her example, pitching his voice loud enough to hear over the wind and low waves, but not so loud he startled their quarry. "I found it in a book by Lefty Kruh. He made it look easy enough."

"Kreh," Jess corrected. "Lefty's the whole reason you're standing here."

Dan let his confusion show.

"Before he came along, fly fishing was pretty much limited to streams and lakes." Jess dipped her rod, a sign of respect for the man who'd brought the sport into salt water. "You're doing a good job, by the way. Especially in this breeze."

Dan grinned. The words were high praise for a guy who, six weeks earlier, had barely known which end of the fly rod to hold. Back then, he'd needed her hands-on instruction. Now, thanks to her lessons, he and Jess fished shoulder to shoulder in water that covered the hem of his shorts and lapped against her waist.

That wasn't the only progress they'd made. Since that night in her apartment, it had been harder and harder for them to resist their attraction to each other. He'd tried. Oh, had he tried. But no matter how far apart from her he vowed he'd stay, somehow, they ended up in each other's arms. With all they had against them, a real relationship still seemed impossible. And the idea that he might be dangerously close to falling head over heels for Jess sent a tremor through fingers that were normally rock-steady.

He scuffed his boot against the riverbed, sending up a plume of sand and grit. He looked down and saw too much thin green cord floating at his side, a rookie mistake that was sure to draw a comment from his teacher. There was only one way to recover—change flies and hope Jess thought that had been his plan all along.

He spun the noisy crank, reloading his reel so the line wouldn't tangle, and braced for constructive criticism. When Jess didn't offer it, he glanced her way and saw she was on her cell phone, her back to him. The reprieve gave him time to choose the right fly for the situation. He studied the cloudy water, wanting to demonstrate all he'd learned.

Gray skies lowered the visibility. The light chop had disturbed a layer of silt and turned the river murky. The outline of the wreck had blurred. He thought fish might have problems seeing the fly and, trying not to read too much into the seductive name, tugged a red-and-white seaducer from a patch of nubby cotton on his vest.

"I told you, that won't work for me."

Jess's voice bounced off the waves. The sharp tone drew his attention. Her shoulders, which always felt so soft under his caress, looked stiff and unyielding.

"Pick a different day. Any other day that week."

His head bent low over his work, he muttered, "Give in, buster." While he clipped off the old fly and tied on a new one, he listened more closely than he intended to one side of a conversation that sounded all too familiar. Though Jess had more good qualities than he could count, meeting someone halfway wasn't one of them. He wondered if anyone had ever explained to her that the *c* in "customer service" stood for compromise. From the way she spoke to someone who sounded suspiciously like a potential client, he thought not.

"Trouble?" he asked after the call ended and Jess faced him again.

"A guy from New York. Comes down every year. He'll be in town for weeks, but only the last Wednesday of the month will do." The frown she wore turned into a teasing grin. She aimed her trigger finger his way. "I told him I had a previous commitment, but he didn't want to hear it. What is wrong with these people?"

The solution was obvious. "He can take my slot," he offered. "You can tack on a makeup lesson at the end of my ten weeks."

She shrugged. "I already told him, no."

It was his turn to frown. He summoned up his sternest voice to say, "Business must be getting better." When Jess toyed with her fly reel instead of answering, he got to the point. "You realize you did the same thing to me, don't you? I think you're worth it, but some customers will just find another guide."

"I won't let them walk all over me," she said, refusing to meet his eyes.

He blew air across his lips. The woman could teach mountains a thing or two about immobility. "I'm not saying you have to be available 24/7. Or skip Adam's birthday party." He smiled to show that last part was a joke. "But maybe if you set limits—be firm, but be fair—more people will hire you. You did say you're trying to rebuild your client list, didn't you?"

Jess didn't answer. She didn't bite his head off, either. All things considered, he chalked up her reaction as progress and made another cast.

"Fish on!" he yelled when the line went tight seconds after the colorful lure hit the water. While Jess watched in silence, he coaxed a nice-size snook from beneath the old boat.

"What are you using?" she asked, once he'd released the fish.

He waggled his eyebrows and dangled the streamer he'd tied the night before. "Want one?" he asked. "It'll cost ya."

A saucy grin formed on her perfect lips, and Jess eased through the water to his side. She palmed the fly while he held his breath. It was one thing to make a good cast or catch a fish, quite another for one of his creations to pass her inspection.

"Sweet," she pronounced. "You're a world-class fly tier. If you ever want to change professions, I could put you to work."

One thing about Jess, she could say the right thing, make him feel prouder, more deserving. There might be times when the boulder-size chip on her shoulder caused problems, but he was willing to whittle away at it. Neither of them was perfect, after all. He bent and brushed his lips over hers.

"Sorry," he murmured. "Already got a job. Which I have to get to in another twenty minutes."

She glided through the water, back to where she'd been standing, while he sent another cast flying toward a white shape that hovered in the wreck's shadows. Jess tucked her rod under her arm and the pout she'd worn earlier turned into a full-fledged frown when a second snook hit his line.

"You are *so* giving me that fly," she said with a smile that warmed his heart.

JESS MUSTERED HER MOST CONGENIAL expression and looked up from the display of line nippers she was re-stocking when the door to On The Fly opened. The edges of her smile turned brittle as she waited for a rotund figure to make his way across the polished oak floor. She'd hoped for an easy start to her campaign to raise money for Connections House, but George Thompson would be anything but easy. On a good day, the man could be pricklier than she was. But she had to take the chance. If she was going to help Dan—and have any hope of a relationship with him—she'd need a lot more than a fundraising label taped to a Mason jar beside the cash register.

She needed the support of the real movers and shakers in the county. The money men. Most of whom, at one time or another, dropped a wad of cash on supplies at On The Fly. Since George definitely fit the bill, Jess brightened her smile and forced her shoulders square.

"Afternoon, George," she said.

"Sam around?" The retired CEO swiveled a shiny bald head to survey the shop.

"Not today. Can I help you?"

"Nah," George said. "Tell him I stopped by, will you?"

When George remained where he was, she stepped from behind the counter. Unless he'd walked through the shop's doors by mistake, the man wanted something. Fly-tying materials lined the back wall, and she narrowed in on the section that held George's interest. "Are you planning to fish some freshwater?"

With a look that was just shy of a grimace, George nodded. "Yeah. I guess." He lifted his chin and pointed. "Sam told me I needed cork to make some poppers. You know where it is?"

"Sure." She led the way to the section he wanted. "We have plenty in stock. What color did you have in mind?"

"Red, I think." He grabbed a small bag of painted cork bodies.

Yellow was Dan's go-to color. She rubbed a finger over lips he had kissed every time he caught a fish and tapped a package of marigold pieces. "I had good luck with this the other day."

George hesitated only a second before slipping the bag from the rack, and Jess widened her stance to keep herself upright. The last time the man had followed her advice, the granddaddy of all trout had been a small fry. Refusing to let her surprise show, she asked, "Are you planning to paint the eyes or glue them on? How 'bout some rubber legs?"

"Yeah, I need all that stuff," George admitted. "Maybe I should get a basket."

She picked one up from a strategically placed stack. "So, what are you making these for? A special fishing trip?" She could scarcely believe the grin that split George's face as they moved on to a selection of feathers.

"My daughter's coming in for a week." His chest puffed out. "Grampa gets to take the grandkids on their first fishing trip. 'Course, we're not going out on the boat," he frowned. "I think I could handle them, but my wife says the three little munchkins would be too much, even for me."

Wise woman.

"There's nothing like your first fish," she said agreeably. "You'll have a blast. And so will the kids." Her smile warmed as she recalled the latest addition to the photo array in her office and Dan's silly grin. "I took a client to the ponds off Pluckebaum the other day. You know that area on the west side of Rockledge? Lots of shallow water makes it a great place for children."

She tried not to laugh when George looked at her as if she'd sprouted a second head. True, she normally kept her best fishing holes a closely guarded secret, but a grandfather who spent time with his grandchildren deserved to shine. She waited for the man's gaping mouth to close before she continued.

"We had good luck there. Caught some bream, even a couple of small bass. 'Course their mouths were larger than their bodies, but kids would get a kick out of that."

"Thanks, Jess," George murmured. Something that looked a whole lot like gratitude shone in the man's blue eyes. "I'll keep it in mind."

They spent the next half hour tossing supplies into his basket before a contented George stood opposite her at the cash register. Looking for an opening, she realized the man was about to leave and she hadn't even broached the most important topic of the day. She stalled for time by asking, "Do you have pictures?"

George's smile brightened. "Do I?" He quickly pulled photos from his wallet and slapped them on the counter. Three tiny faces—one Asian, one Hispanic, one Black—smiled up at Jess.

"They're beautiful, George. How old are they?"

George pointed a stubby finger at the oldest. "An," he said, rhyming the name with *yawn,* "is six." Four-year-old Mateo was next in line, followed by the baby of the family, three-year-old Taj who, according to the man on the other side of the counter, did his best to live up to his Urdu name for "exalted one."

"You must be very proud," she said as she watched her customer's reaction closely. "Of your daughter and son-in-law, *and* their children."

"I sure am." If possible, George's chest puffed out a little further.

"The need is tremendous. Everywhere." She gestured to the four walls. "You ever consider doing something about it right here? On Merritt Island?"

"I'm too old to be a dad again," George guffawed. "Other than giving to my church, I'm not sure I could be of much help."

"I might know a way," she said and somehow managed to sound as though she wasn't personally invested in the outcome of the conversation. "A friend of mine, a local doctor, plans to build a housing complex for teens who grew up in the foster care system. As usual, money's a problem, but I think you'd be impressed with his ideas."

When George's eyes didn't glaze over, she kept going, filling him in on the plans and letting her own enthusiasm for the project show. Twenty minutes and several questions later, she finished up with, "I'd really like you to meet him."

George searched her face. "You say he's from around here?"

"Yup. Dan Hamilton. Thoracic surgeon. He was a foster kid himself, so he understands the scope of the problem." When George seemed to waver, she added, "Sam likes him."

The recommendation tipped the scales in the direction she'd hoped they would go.

"Let me run it by the gang at Jimmies," George said. The county's most influential people sat down for breakfast at the family diner every Thursday. "If I can get some others interested, I'll get in touch to set up a meeting with your doctor friend."

After a few more minutes of chitchat, George headed out the door, leaving Jess to stare after him. She shook her head. Who would have guessed that underneath the man's pompous exterior lay the tender heart of a grandfather and philanthropist? She returned to the box of nippers she'd been sorting, but her hand stilled.

She'd always assumed George was just a grouchy old man, but what if the problem was really in the way *she* looked at people? Was that what Sam had been trying to tell her? And hadn't Dan said practically the same thing? Maybe George wasn't the only customer she'd misjudged. She'd been so cold to Dan when they first met, it was a wonder the man didn't have freezer burn.

The question was, why? She hadn't always been this way. In On The Fly's early years, she'd recognized the occasional urge to snap at a customer and stifled it. All that had changed with Tom's death. She'd grown bitter, and she hadn't tried to hide it. Tears stung her eyes as she realized that resentment had been a way of holding on to her anger over the way her husband had died.

The time had come to let go of the past and move forward. Yes, preserving Phelps Cove was as important as it had always been. That was one dream she refused to give up. Not because it was Tom's legacy, but because it was Henry's, and because the habitat was too important to lose.

But there were other ways her life could change and she had a pretty good idea of the direction she wanted one of them to take.

CHRIS WAS ON HIS FEET ALMOST before Dan finished chewing his last bite of chicken. The boy's head brushed against moss that dripped from a low-hanging scrub oak. He batted the coarse gray strands away from his face.

"C'mon," said the teen. "Let's catch us some fish. I'm ready to try out those new flies."

On the other side of a blanket spread across white sand, Sean gave his mouth a rough wipe and balled his napkin. He arced it neatly into a nearby patch of sandspurs.

"Two points." The third voice belonged to Paul who, as the newest member of the group, usually competed with Chris for bragging rights. "Bet I can catch the first fish."

"Hold on." The big guy remained where he was. "Didn't I hear something about brownies?"

Regina elbowed her brother's ribs. "It's always about the food with you, isn't it?"

"Food and basketball, little sis. Food and basketball." Sean wadded up another napkin and sent it flying.

Elbows on cross-legged knees, Regina hunched over, making herself smaller. The tiny lines that bracketed the girl's mouth deepened. "You don't like fishing?" she worried.

Sean draped one long arm around her shoulders while he helped himself to a handful of chocolate from the box being passed around. "Relax." He gave her a gentle shake. "I'm here, ain't I?"

Dan swept a look at the leftovers from lunch. The cove made the perfect spot to take a crew whose weekly lessons had progressed to fishing from the shore. Plus, he thought the teens might like to see the future site of The Aegean. Not that he'd gotten around to discussing the latter. So far, the day had been all about food. Store-bought potato salad and baked beans had disappeared nearly as fast as Maddy's home-fried chicken, but plastic containers and paper plates littered the picnic area. Dan cleared his throat. "Nobody fishes till we clean up all this mess."

Around him, five faces registered confusion.

"What for, Doc? In case you didn't notice, we be outside," Chris objected.

"We *are* outside," Dan corrected. "Sitting here on this nice beach." His nod took in the river scant yards away. He pointed to scruffy-looking oaks and the stand of waxy mangroves beyond. "Trees all around. Not a speck of trash in sight. That is, not counting Sean's contribution. You want to get those, son." He aimed a no-nonsense look at the teen who served as role model for all the others. "My fly fishing instructor, Jess, says it's important to leave the area as clean as you find it. Maybe even cleaner. We don't want anyone to know we've been here."

The time Paul had spent on the streets showed in the searching look he whipped behind him. When no one stepped from behind the nearest tree and began questioning his right to be where he was, he swung back to face Dan. "You said it was okay to be here, right?"

"It's fine, but that's not the point. Jess says we should take care of the outdoors like it was our own backyard." He sent another nod Sean's way.

"If you say so," the teen agreed with a resigned sigh. He unfolded his muscular legs and headed for the paper wads among the weeds.

"Damn." He stuck one finger in his mouth. "They's thorns." A little more cautiously, he plucked the napkins from between needle-sharp prickers using his other hand.

Jose grabbed a couple of paper plates. Consternation puckered his brow. "Where's the trash can?"

"I brought trash bags," Dan answered. "We'll toss 'em in the garbage back at the house."

"Good plan, Doc," Jose agreed.

With everyone pitching in, the cleanup tasks were completed in practically no time. Dan gave the area a final once-over, deciding it would meet Jess's high standards, before he let Regina and the boys grab fly rods and assorted equipment from the trunk of his car. As they had the week before when he'd taken the group fishing at a small pond, they spread out along the water's edge, each far enough from their neighbor that no one had to worry about being hooked by, or hooking, a buddy. Regina chose the spot closest to her brother, where she made several flawless casts that were the envy of all the boys. Sean, Chris and Jose managed to get their lines wet soon after, but Paul struggled, and Dan stopped to help his least experienced pupil.

"You're trying too hard." He grasped the young man's elbow and walked him through the motions for making a cast the same way Jess had taught him. The boy caught on quickly and soon placed the fly twenty yards out. Paul's proud grin made giving up another Sunday afternoon to work with the boys and Regina worthwhile.

Dan made his way down the line, offering correction and advice where necessary. He kept a wary eye on Regina who turned away from the water and stepped to a jumble of fallen rocks and tree limbs while he gave Sean a few pointers. When something rustled in the bushes at the top of the rise, Dan left off in midsentence and moved quickly, his footsteps slowing only as he recognized the raspy calls of several sandhill cranes.

"Regina, you don't want to feed those birds." Careful not to startle the cranes or the girl, he looked pointedly at a small mound of brown crumbs that trailed from the foot of the hill.

"Why not?" Regina kicked sand to hide the evidence. "They sound hungry."

"Maybe they are, but we don't know what to feed them."

"Everybody likes brownies." The girl smiled broadly and held out her hand. A good-size chunk of the treat she'd saved from lunch filled her palm.

"You should eat that yourself. Or save it for later. It might make the birds sick." When Regina gave him a questioning look, he added, "Jess says that if wild animals get used to eating our food and stop looking for their own, they'll get fat and lazy. Then, what happens if no one comes out here to feed them?"

"I could take them home with me," she said, hopeful.

"I'm pretty sure the birds need to stay here. They probably have a nest close by, and they'd miss their friends if they had to move." His argument struck a little too close to home for both of them. He fumbled for another answer. Large, squawking birds gave him an idea. "I'm sure Mrs. Shea wouldn't want such noisy pets."

"You're probably right, but I like 'em," Regina mumbled. She tamped the crumbs deeper into the sand. "They sound like those dumb instruments we used in elementary school. The wooden tube with the stick."

"Tone blocks," he said, smiling at the memory. "And you're right."

Finished with the birds, Regina's attention shifted elsewhere. "Is Jess your girlfriend?" she asked as she prepared to cast.

"My—" Where had that come from? "No, she's teaching me how to use a fly rod. The same way I'm teaching you." He studied the river, hoping for fish, or even a stingray, anything to distract the girl.

"You sure talk about her an awful lot," she insisted. The fly at the end of her line sailed over the water.

He absorbed the comment while he watched Regina strip line and make another cast. She was right about one thing—the words he'd used today had been his own, but it was Jess's voice he'd heard in his head when he'd said them. It seemed as though he'd picked up more than a new skill during his lessons with the feisty fly fisher. He tipped his head back, letting his gaze travel from the clear river up the sandy bluff and over the tangle of bushes and trees beyond.

He closed his eyes, envisioning the land as Jess predicted it would look once The Aegean took over. The river bottom, muddied from dredging. The water, slicked with oil and gasoline from visiting yachts. Trash strewn along the shoreline. Trees and brush clear-cut to make way for the clinic and housing. A parking lot instead of an orange grove.

On the hill above him, the cranes moved away from the edge, their deep, stuttering caws fading.

When construction demolished their nests, what would happen to the sandhills? Or all the other animals that lived in the hundred-acre parcel? As Bryce had pointed out, this was the last undeveloped acreage on Merritt Island—where else could they go?

Dan shook his head to clear his thoughts. Backing out of the development would jeopardize everything. Not only Connections House, but his standing among his peers. A standing that guaranteed the security he'd always wanted.

And yet, could he really be a part of the destruction of Phelps Cove?

A sudden bend in Regina's rod tip saved him from answering. The girl yelped and Dan smiled broadly, glad she'd gotten the first strike. She handled the fish on the line precisely as she'd been told and, without a single reminder, quickly landed a small trout.

"Oh, man! Fish for dinner," Chris called. He reeled in quickly and threw another cast. "I'm next."

Dan let his voice carry along the shore to Jose who stood the farthest away. "Jess—" At Regina's smug glance, he stopped and started over.

"Smart fly fishermen practice catch-and-release, so we won't be taking any fish home with us." Certain his next idea would override the moans and groans that rose from the group, he added, "But I'll spring for supper at Long John Silver's, and I brought a camera."

The pictures kept everyone honest as the boys and Regina traded fish stories over dinner.

By six, when he'd dropped everyone off, Dan was headed for home with plans for a shower, a beer and an early night. Plans that faded as he absently pushed the

Replay button on his answering machine. Jess's cryptic message about a meeting Wednesday night deserved a follow-up phone call, but the next two messages were more recent and more pressing. He checked the cell phone, which hadn't buzzed once while he was at Phelps Cove. His voicemail box was full and he cursed the vagaries of intermittent coverage while he bolted for the door, all thoughts of an early evening giving way to the needs of his patients.

Chapter Eleven

Dan punched his speed dial and, on each step that led to his parking space, fired off questions at the attending.

"How many are hurt? What's the extent of the injuries? Do we have X-rays? MRIs?"

"It's a madhouse," answered the emergency room physician. "One DOA and four in serious condition. Two, critical. The first is on his way to the O.R. now. Test results will be waiting for you when you get here. The trauma team is working to stabilize the other one."

He slipped behind the wheel of his car and sped out of the parking lot. Living so close to the hospital meant that in ten life-saving minutes, he was pelting down the hallway toward a bank of elevators. Two minutes after that, he stepped into the scrub area adjacent to the operating room. Lab work and scans hung over the sink. He studied while he washed and, when he had absorbed the facts and figures, he backed into a green-tiled room where the surgical staff stood like actors on a set. Frozen, they waited for a director to yell, "Action."

And here he came.

Beneath his ribs, moths beat their wings. The breeze

of self-doubt that rose before every surgery whispered through him. Statistics said someone from his background should be slinging burgers in a fast-food joint. Not the top guy in a demanding field where lives were at stake. Yet, with luck and hard work, he'd altered his fate. He drew himself marginally straighter, his doubts settling before the door whispered shut.

"Let's begin, shall we?" He took the scalpel proffered by a surgical nurse and lowered his hands to the patient's chest.

Three hours later, Dan stepped back to let another nurse wipe his brow. Now that the dicey surgery was nearly over, he eyed the face of the patient on his operating table. Acne marred the boy's teenage cheeks, and wisps of sandy-blond hair had escaped his scrub cap. The fine features and coloring reminded him of Adam, and a fierce protectiveness tightened his gut.

As he worked, he asked, "What do we hear from the E.R.?"

"The other chest injury, a sixteen-year-old male, is in O.R. Two. It's been touch and go—he coded twice—and Dr. Chase asked how soon you can step in. Says to make it sooner rather than later."

"Chase, huh?" He gave a quick nod of assent. "Let him know we're wrapping up. I'll be there shortly."

While he closed the incision, he wondered if anyone else realized the significance of having the other thoracic surgeon ask for him by name. The request definitely elevated his status. Until now, he'd been thinking that the recognition and success he craved would only come through acceptance in the right social circles, at the right events. But here, where it counted, his skill and dedication were doing the job by themselves.

"Who was driving?" he asked as the surgical assistant covered the wound. From the kid's injuries, he knew his patient hadn't been behind the wheel.

A nurse answered. "DOA, doctor."

Such a waste.

His jaw clenched as he considered that vehicle accidents took the lives of more young adults than any other cause of death. Not so terribly far in the future, Adam would slip behind the wheel of a car. Though Jess did a superb job of mothering the boy, Dan wanted to be there to help warn him about dangerous distractions, driving too fast, drinking. To remind the little guy to keep his grades up, be kind to his mother and cover all the other bases a dad usually handled.

His breath stilled. He'd had a few "uncles" in his life, men who hung around long enough to earn a seat at the Sunday-morning breakfast table. Once or twice he'd dreamed of a stepdad who would take him to baseball games or on camping trips, but his mom's boyfriends had never lasted. Before he'd learned to keep his guard up, he'd felt the sting of abandonment when they stopped coming around. He wouldn't do that to Adam. The boy deserved better. But was he really thinking of commitment here?

Suddenly, having a permanent place in the child's life was something he knew he wanted.

The same way he knew he wanted Jess.

He'd fallen in love with her. She could take him down a peg or two with that cheeky attitude of hers, but her strong sense of independence kept his need for control in check. And while it was true she didn't move in the same social circles as his doctor friends, that wasn't nearly as important as the forever kind of love he thought they could have together.

If they could set aside their differences over Phelps Cove.

To make that happen, one of them had to give. And since the land couldn't move, The Aegean group would have to. In the weeks he'd been fishing with Jess, he'd come to appreciate the stretch of pristine Florida wilderness she so jealously guarded. And, for the first time, he realized it was his job to compromise.

JESS PULLED THE LAST OF THE fly rods from the box that had arrived with the morning's UPS shipment. She held the limber graphite out straight and gave it a twitch, smiling when the tip flexed smoothly. Her smile deepened when the phone rang and the display screen told her it was Bob Richards. The legislature was in full swing, and the funding bill for Phelps Cove had finally made the agenda. With all her work to preserve the land about to be rewarded, she lunged for the phone.

"Bob, give me the good word and I'll break out the champagne." There was a bottle chilling in the bottom drawer of her refrigerator, just waiting for the right occasion.

"I'm afraid I have bad news," he said with the somber tone of a funeral director.

The rod she'd been so happy with clattered into the shipping crate as Jess sank onto her chair. She listened, her unease growing, as Bob explained that things in Tallahassee had taken an unexpected turn. The finance committee had demanded a balanced budget before the legislature considered any new business. With only a few weeks remaining before the session ended, the purchase of Phelps Cove probably wouldn't make it to the floor.

That left only one option—go back to Henry's niece and ask her to extend their contract.

"That's our only choice?" The heiress had sworn to fight the state's purchase of Phelps Cove. She was unlikely to grant Jess or POE any favors, especially this one.

"'Fraid so. How soon can you talk to her?"

"We're having lunch after Henry's memorial on Friday." She'd made reservations at a four-star restaurant in Cocoa Village.

Over the next couple of days, Jess devoted all her free time to preparing for the talk with Estelle Phelps. But on Wednesday, she shoved aside her worries about the cove long enough to ready On The Fly for another important meeting, this one with George and his friends. Soon, upholstered chairs and ottomans circled the wooden table where customers often studied charts of local waters. As Jess swept reference guides out of sight, replacing them with platters of cheese puffs and cookies, worry slowed her steps. She and Dan had been playing phone tag for the past few days, something that hadn't concerned her until he'd cancelled this morning's fly fishing lesson. She looped her finger through a curl and tugged. Everything was moving so quickly, she hadn't had a chance to go over her ideas for Connections House with him.

A short time later, when she still hadn't been able to reach Dan and everyone else had arrived, Jess plastered an assured look over mounting apprehension and stole a peek into the shop's cozy book nook. Her gaze closed in on Florida's fifth-richest woman. Had she actually seen the woman squirrel away cookies in her purse? As hard as it was to believe, the telltale corner of a napkin protruded from her Gucci bag.

And napkins didn't lie.

Jess turned away, warding off a nervous urge to laugh. Instead, she made a show of straightening her wristwatch to cover the fact that she was really checking the time.

Five past the hour.

Cold swirled into the room as the door of the shop opened to admit the man she'd been waiting for. When his eyes met hers, his lips curved into a distant relative of his usual smile. The creases around his mouth and at the corners of his eyes had deepened. Damp hair curled at his collar and day-old stubble shadowed his jaw. The instant he spotted the knot of people behind her, he hesitated.

"What's going on?"

"In here." She hustled them into an alcove where fishing vests hung from wooden rods. If she had timed it right, she'd have about thirty seconds before an eager guest or two descended. And if she was very lucky, Dan would forgive her for the spot she'd landed him in.

"I've been trying to reach you all week," she said quickly. She stared into eyes that looked impossibly older than their thirty-five years. Fatigue had etched lines into his forehead. She fought the urge to rub his temples, keeping her fingers in check by smoothing them over her own hair. A bobby pin had worked loose and she pushed it back into place.

Dan shook his head. "Sorry. There was a bad accident Sunday afternoon. I've been wrestling a couple of young patients back from death's door ever since, and I've barely left the hospital."

"They'll be okay?" she asked.

"Looks like they'll pull through." He ran his long, slender fingers over his face and stretched, rolling his broad shoulders.

Another time, another place and Jess might have offered him a back rub. As it was, the close quarters made it hard enough to resist kissing him.

"I'm sorry to spring this on you. If I'd known, I would have rescheduled." She stopped, unable to fault him for not dropping everything to call her when lives depended on his skill and dedication. "If you're not up for this, I suppose we could put it off." She tugged her bottom lip between her teeth. "Only we might not get another chance."

"Maybe you should tell me what *this* is first." Dan studied her, perplexed.

"I invited some of my customers and their friends to hear you talk about Connections House."

"What?" He stepped back. "Why?"

The question deserved an honest answer. What had started off as a way to eliminate his challenge for Phelps Cove had turned into so much more.

"I wanted to give us a chance," she said, clasping her hands to still her trembling fingers. "It seemed like the only way to make it happen."

There was more, but an impatient George had found them so the rest would have to wait until later, when she and Dan were alone. Assuming he was still speaking to her by then.

Turning, she introduced him to the man who wore a tattered fishing shirt and shorts. She tried not to think about first impressions as she stepped aside.

"So, Dan," George began once hands had been shaken and names traded. "Jess has told us that you have a plan to help older teens. We've talked among ourselves." He gestured to the others, who had settled into comfortable chairs. "We agree that you've identified a growing problem. We'd like to hear what you have to say and see if there's some way for us to participate."

"Now, wait a minute," interrupted a woman whose two-inch gray roots belied the fact that she owned half of downtown Cocoa. "I'm all for giving folks a leg up. But I quit hiring these kids. They don't stick around. They're here one day." Cheryl waved a hand. "The next, they're a no-show."

The woman couldn't have provided a better opening if Jess had planned it herself. She watched Dan take a second to gather his thoughts before he launched into an effortless description of the problems faced by young adults who aged out of the foster care system. When he finished, the people around the table wore concerned frowns. A spate of intelligent questions erupted. Equally insightful answers followed. When the room fell silent, Jess held her breath until Marge pulled a steno pad and a stubby pencil from the depths of her purse.

"Well, let's see what we can come up with," she announced.

"I think that motel in Angel City might work," suggested Charley Combs. Beneath a work-worn chambray shirt and farmer's tan beat the heart of one of the county's biggest property owners. "It's been sitting vacant the last couple of years. Without too much effort, I think we could renovate it. What do you think, Dan? A motel, as a place to start?"

With a sharp inhale, Dan swung to face Jess. Amusement danced in the wide-eyed look he gave her before composure settled over his features and he faced Charley again. "Uh, yeah," he said. "We could work with that."

A local builder straightened his dapper bow tie and leaned away from the side conversation he'd been having with George. "I can lend a construction crew till fall when the housing market picks up. I'll scrounge around for building materials and paint. Won't cost us a cent."

"If there's rewiring to be done, call my office." At the far end of the table, the speaker pulled the latest in cell phone gadgets from a hip pocket and tapped some keys. "I'll send Gus a reminder."

"That takes care of the building," Marge announced. "What else do we need? Furniture? Small appliances?"

"I have beds, tables and chairs in storage." Charley crossed one booted foot over the other. "We'd need new mattresses. Microwaves might be nice."

"I'll donate those," offered a man whose discount appliance stores advertised heavily on Sunday-morning television.

Marge ticked two more items off her list.

"And I can handle window coverings and linens," said Cheryl. "How many units are we talking about?"

"Thirty," someone said.

The look on his face said Dan wasn't accustomed to the warp-speed at which plans were being made, but he still managed to interject, "I thought we'd start off with a smaller group. Say, half that many?"

"Well, sure," George agreed. "That means one wing for classrooms, a main living area, maybe a gym. We'd turn the other wing into fifteen apartments. Small, but livable."

"And a suite for the caretakers," Dan added. "My foster parents, Glen and Maddy Hollis, said they'd get the house up and running. They're doing the same thing now on a much smaller scale."

"An excellent choice," said George while Marge scribbled notes. More nods followed. The Hollises were well-known and highly regarded members of the community. "Now, you mentioned classes. GED? College prep? Tutors? That sort of thing?"

Dan leaned forward. "You'd be surprised how few basic life skills these kids pick up in school."

The bank president nodded. "Show me a high school student who rectifies monthly statements, and I'll throw in another thousand bucks."

Marge peered over her wire-rimmed glasses. "One thousand for incidentals. Okay. So, how about food? If they're anything like my teenagers, even boiling water is a challenge."

Earning a chuckle or two, the owner of half of the county's fast-food restaurants said he'd send his personal chef and a nutritionist to provide tips on preparing simple, inexpensive meals. The Chevy dealer offered a mechanic who could teach the importance of oil changes and tire rotation. That led to a conversation about driving lessons, since the schools no longer offered free driver education. Jobs were next on the agenda, and options were being considered when Dan's pager went off.

Looking at the screen, he grimaced. "Sorry. I'm needed back at the hospital."

"Well, I think we've made a good start." George slapped an open palm against his thigh. He scooted his chair back and stood. "We'll get moving on this and hammer out the rest of the details as we go along, but I don't see any reason why we shouldn't be able to open the doors by the first of the year, do you?"

A chorus of "sounds good" and "okay by me" rose above the scrape of chair legs and the gathering of belongings.

"Eventually, we'll need a lawyer to make sure we're

legal. And we probably ought to involve someone from Family Services. But, Dan, this is still your baby. We want you to run point on it."

Dan's Adam's apple bobbed up and down. "I can't tell you how much this means." His voice thickened. "How much it will mean to kids growing up in foster care."

Though he swept the room, meeting the eyes of every person there, Jess warmed when his gaze lingered on her. As she watched Dan head out the door minutes later, her heart beat with the realization that the handsome doctor's whole life was aimed at saving others, and that somewhere between his arrival and departure she'd fallen hopelessly in love with the man.

HIS LEGS STRETCHED OUT BENEATH his desk, Dan stretched to relieve a sharp pain in his foot. He'd been in surgery all day, so it would have been easy to tell himself the strain was natural. Trouble was, he knew tension, not fatigue, had caused the muscle cramp.

"I think I have a problem with The Aegean group," he said, finally getting around to the reason he'd asked Glen to drop by his office. Across from him, Glen's bushy eyebrows rose.

"You think? Or you know?"

"Pretty sure I do," Dan admitted. He passed a pen back and forth between his hands. "The upshot is, I changed my mind about developing Phelps Cove."

Glen leaned back in his chair, his arms folded across his chest. "That's not going to make your new friends very happy. What made you switch sides?"

"As funny as it sounds, taking fishing lessons to get ready for that Belize trip has given me a new appreciation for our natural resources." He held the pen like a fly rod and pretended to cast. "And since Phelps Cove

is one of the area's last stretches of undeveloped land..."
He flicked his wrist, confident that Glen would connect
the dots.

"Ironic," the older man said. "Have you broken it to
them yet?"

"I'll talk to Bryce after the card game Saturday night.
Suggest they find a new place." Thanks to Jess, he had
a few ideas. All along the river, crumbling tear-downs
waited for someone to come along and raze the older
homes to build anew. If the development team strung a
few of those properties together, The Aegean could find
another location. The plan had merit. And according to
Bryce, Phelps Cove hadn't been his first choice.

"If they don't go for it, I'll back out of the surgical
center."

Glen slipped into his usual role of the devil's ad-
vocate. "Have you thought this through? Figured out
how far back it'll push the timetable for Connections
House?"

Dan went back to passing the pen from hand to hand.
"Actually, we might open sooner rather than later."

He explained about the meeting at On The Fly.
"Would you have a problem if there were a lot more
people involved?"

Dan held his breath and braced for objections.

Glen leaned back in the chair nearest the desk and
crossed his booted feet. "Truthfully, I never felt it should
be a one-man show," he announced.

At the droll statement Dan missed the pen. It clattered
to the floor.

"Really," he said, trying not to sound as insulted as
he felt.

"Don't get your shorts in a bind," Glen said, his
wrinkles curving up. "No one is more eager than I am

to help these kids get on their feet. But for a project like this to succeed, it needs community support, community financing. I went along with your plans because I know you. Once you get your mind made up about something, there isn't any stopping you. But this— You can't do it all yourself. I wondered when you'd figure it out."

As usual, Glen had his best interests at heart. Since he'd never envisioned the project as the Dan Hamilton house, his demeanor softened. After a short review of the details, the conversation turned to life in Glen and Maddy's household and dinner on Sunday.

On his way out a few minutes later, the retired foster dad stopped to rest his hand on the door frame. "I figure it took someone mighty special to change your mind about The Aegean project. My money's on that fly fishing guide you've been spending time with. She must care about you an awful lot to go to this much trouble." Glen's words slowed. "Doesn't she have a kid? Have you given any thought to him?"

"His name's Adam." Dan nodded, not at all surprised that Glen knew all about Jess and her son. By now, his foster parents had probably discussed which college the boy would attend. "We're taking things slow."

The pace they'd set was practically glacial. But was there any other choice?

"Sounds like you don't need my advice." The older man paused, then added, "You're gonna get it anyway. You probably don't want to let someone like that get away. Hang on to her, son."

"I'll give it my best," he whispered to the vacant doorway.

Chapter Twelve

Friday afternoon, Jess rose to greet Estelle Phelps as the woman strode into the best restaurant in Brevard County. Henry had always said his niece deserved an F in "shares well with others." Jess intended to turn that grade into an A when it came to Phelps Cove. But if Estelle's thinly pursed lips were any indication, she had a tough job ahead of her.

"Estelle, thank you for meeting me. I know this can't be an easy day for you, what with the service and all. It was a lovely memorial." Even though, judging from the mistakes he'd made in the eulogy, the minister hadn't known Henry any better than his niece had.

Estelle gave her proffered hand a limp shake. "So nice to finally meet you. I missed you in the receiving line."

"I couldn't stay," Jess murmured. If she'd been stronger, she might have stuck around. But one look at the heavy oak pew where she'd sat during Tom's funeral, one whiff of the same cloying floral scent, and it had been all she could do to hold herself together through the benediction.

"Too bad," Estelle said with a sigh. "We could have talked there and avoided—" she swept a scathing glare over rosebud wallpaper and tasseled draperies "—all this."

The remark dimmed Jess's hopes of establishing some kind of rapport with Henry's niece. She watched Estelle stretch a languid hand over her glass just as the waiter began to pour.

"I prefer bottled water," the woman informed him without so much as a glance in his direction. "From a mountain spring. You do carry premium brands, don't you?" She tossed a doubtful look his way.

"Yes, madam," assured the formally attired man while Estelle leaned back to let another of the staff spread a linen napkin across her lap. "Of course."

Seconds later, Jess drank deeply from a glass of perfectly fine tap water while the waiter presented a cobalt-blue bottle as if it were fine wine. He poured. Estelle tasted. She nodded, though a marginal lift of one starched eyebrow made it clear the selection—and the menu choices—fell below her usual standard. After grilling him at length on sauces and specials, she ordered an ordinary Caesar salad.

"The duck," Jess said, opting for the restaurant's signature dish. She smiled her thanks to their waiter as she handed him the leather-bound menu.

Once they were alone, she launched into a speech so well practiced she could recite it while balancing her checkbook. "POE would like to name the Phelps Cove Visitor Center in your honor. Think of it. Every person who comes—" She faltered when Estelle waved her hand.

"And in exchange?"

Jess muffled a sigh. "In exchange, you'd give us an extension on Henry's contract. We're asking for a couple of months, tops. On the other hand, your name on the center would last forever."

Estelle laughed. "Nice try, but no. As I told you the last time we spoke, I'm not interested in posterity. *Money* talks." Shaking her head, she passed a butter knife over a pot of the restaurant's famed cheese spread and dabbed a transparent film across a slice of fragrant rye toast. "I'll never understand my uncle's obsession with that swamp."

Jess eyed the bread. In her rush to get out of the house this morning, she'd skipped breakfast. But much as she wanted to help herself, talking with her mouth full was not an option. Especially since she'd just been given the opening she needed.

"It's not a swamp." She rubbed her damp fingers on the hem of her napkin. "It's a beautiful piece of land that borders on a premier habitat for trout and redfish. The acreage itself is home to everything from songbirds to bobcats. An old orange grove dates back to the 1800s. To preserve its history, POE will salvage timbers from the sharecropper's cabin. I'd love to show you all of our plans and take you on a tour of the property. I'll even take you fishing there if you'd like."

"No, no." Estelle broke her slice of toast into four pieces and set them on her bread plate without taking so much as a nibble. "I couldn't possibly fit it into my schedule." She tossed her glossy black hair over her shoulder and straightened the collar of a perfectly tailored white blouse. "Though if the land is as lovely as you describe, it's no wonder I've received several inquiries about it. One group in particular has offered to more than double the state's offer." She nudged the bread plate to one side.

"The Aegean?" Jess asked drily.

"Oh." A newfound respect filled the look Estelle turned on her. "So you know about them, do you?"

Jess put extra effort into making her tone reasonable. "You know, your uncle wanted to preserve the land."

"My uncle wanted me—and my children—to be well provided for." Estelle lifted her head and looked down her nose. "For their sakes, I can't afford to sell for less than the best price. Besides, there's no guarantee the state will honor its part of the agreement."

"Oh, I'm sure they'll come through," Jess insisted. The legislature had delayed their vote, but they hadn't vetoed the funding bill. "We just need a little more time."

Estelle took a very expensive sip of water. "You strike me as an intelligent woman," she said. "You should know that nothing in politics is a lock until the final vote is cast."

A flurry of activity interrupted as their food was served. The rich smell of roast game and cherries wafted up when one of the staff whisked a silver cover from the plate he set in front of Jess. Her mouth watered, and she reached for her knife and fork, determined to enjoy the rare treat before her rumbling stomach proclaimed her hunger to the entire restaurant.

Across the table, Estelle listlessly stirred a fork through her salad before blotting her lips on her napkin. She leaned forward, pinning Jess with a speculative gaze while her voice dropped nearly to a whisper. "Let's be frank, woman to woman, all right?"

Jess gave her food a wistful look before crossing her knife and fork on her plate.

"Every delay in the legislature increases the chances that the interested parties will move on to something else. Since I do not intend to suffer for my uncle's shortsightedness, I'd need your personal guarantee that the state will uphold its end of the bargain before I could even consider turning down this other party's offer."

Certain the conversation had veered into dangerous waters, Jess asked, "And how would I do that?"

"Pony up some serious escrow money," Estelle said, shrugging her thin shoulders. "Give me a show of good faith. You'll get your money back when the deal goes through."

Jess wasn't sure whether she should be intrigued or insulted. Either way, what Estelle was suggesting simply couldn't happen. "I don't have those kind of resources," she scoffed.

"Really?" Estelle's head tilted to the side. "You're a businesswoman, aren't you? You have assets?"

She had On The Fly, but she couldn't risk it. Not even for Phelps Cove. "The shop is my son's future."

"Ah." Estelle nodded and pushed back into her seat. "It's all well and good to make assurances as long as you're not dealing with your own money. And yet, you're asking me to turn away potential buyers."

"Not turn away, exactly. More time—that's all I'm asking for."

When a marginal lift of one finger was Estelle's only answer, Jess prayed her own fraying patience wouldn't snap and searched for an innocuous topic.

"How long will you be in town?"

"Just long enough to take care of Henry's affairs. Maybe a month." Estelle examined one of her nails. Apparently satisfied that the polish hadn't chipped, she let her hand fall to her lap. "Meantime, I'll work on my golf game. Do you play?"

Though she itched to say, "Some of us work for a living," Jess kept her voice neutral. "The shop and my work for POE don't leave much free time. I spend that with my son."

"Ah."

Still hoping to find a soft spot somewhere in Estelle's heart, she continued. "He's five and a bit of a handful, but most boys are. We have a lot of fun to—" A hand on her wrist stopped her.

"Don't despair. He'll outgrow all that and be off on his own in no time."

So much for common ground, Jess thought as she gave up trying to engage the woman and concentrated on her duck. Which, now that it had grown cold, didn't taste nearly as good as it smelled. She managed a bite or two before Estelle pushed her salad aside with a long-suffering sigh.

"In New York," she announced, "Caesar salad is made with coddled eggs and real anchovies." She prodded her plate. "Not paste." Her water glass had gone empty. She tapped the rim with a long tapered nail, and one of their waiters pulled another bottle from the serving cart.

"Honestly," Estelle complained. "I don't know how you drink the water here. It reeks of sulfur."

Jess sipped from her own glass and rolled the clear liquid over her tongue. The only sulfur she tasted came from the she-devil sitting opposite her.

"RAISE YOU TWO HUNDRED."

Bryce flipped a couple of black-edged chips onto the green felt and sank deeper into his club chair. One smoothly manicured pinkie trapped his cards against the table. His other hand dangled, lax, from the armrest, the cigar between his middle and forefinger apparently forgotten. To the casual observer, the head of the medi-

cal society looked as though he didn't have a care in
the world.

Dan knew better.

Having played poker with his business partners twice
a month for the past eight weeks, he'd observed that the
deeper Bryce wallowed in his chair, the crappier his
hand. Unfortunately, a lowly pair of deuces didn't put
Dan in position to take advantage of that insight. He
tossed his cards onto the table, facedown.

"Too rich for my blood."

Out of the action, he watched and waited. Chase
might have dropped out of The Aegean, but his friends
hadn't deserted him. Dan noticed him lick his lips and
eye his bourbon, a sure sign he clutched at least a straight
between his tightly fisted fingers. Ice clinked in Mark's
glass; he had nothing. Beneath the table, Jack uncrossed
his legs before crossing them in the opposite direction.
Nothing there, either. More hands folded as each man
decided to play it safe.

When Chase threw down along with the others, Dan
struggled to maintain a poker face. How was it possible
that Chase hadn't read Bryce's glaring tell? The man
really ought to work on his observation skills. In surgery
as well as at the poker table.

"You made quite a steal," Dan murmured to the
winner. He dropped a quick nod toward the one man
who, from all accounts, could ill-afford the loss.

"Who? Me?" Bryce asked innocently while he
scooped the impressive pot of chips into colorful stacks.
He slugged bourbon, a predatory glint in his eyes disap-
pearing behind the rim of his glass. He puffed on his
cigar, and the pall of smoke over the table thickened.
As everyone anted up and the deal passed to the next
player, the senior man settled his elbows on the table.

"My eyes and ears in the state capitol tell me the legislature has pushed funding for Phelps Cove off the agenda. At least temporarily. My man says if we grease a few of the right palms—" Bryce fanned the cards he'd been dealt, and took a quick look before snapping them into a neat pile. He gave an exaggerated wink. Winked again. "We'll be clearing land by the end of the month. I can count on twenty thousand from each of you, can't I?"

"I'm not sure bribery is such a good idea," Dan managed. He'd expected a few just-one-more-thing's to bump up his investment in The Aegean. This request, however, was way over the line.

"You misunderstand. The head of the finance committee is a close personal friend of mine," Bryce said with feigned innocence. "Unfortunately, he's in a bit of a jam, financially. This is a loan from one pal to another. Just to tide him over."

Mark elbowed Foreman. "Yeah." He grinned. "A loan."

Both men laughed as Foreman nodded. "With a generous repayment schedule."

"And no interest," pointed out Chase, who probably wished for one himself.

"Call it what you want—greasing palms, bribery, whatever—it's not going to look good on the front page of the newspaper," Dan insisted.

Bryce blew out a noisy breath. "You say that as if anyone at this table would put their career on the line by talking too much."

One thing about Bryce, he got right to the point. The man had enough clout to ensure that anyone who talked would be blacklisted for what was left of a very short career in medicine. Though he'd already decided to leave the group, Dan thought a little fence-mending was in order.

"You know how investigative reporters are whenever they find the least discrepancy in a lobbyist's bank account. I wouldn't want to see any of us get tangled up in something that might jeopardize our reputations."

Bryce cocked his head. "You think my man is so stupid he doesn't know how to cover his tracks?"

"I don't know him, so I couldn't say." Dan fanned his cards and casually noted the full house.

"It won't be a problem," Bryce countered with an apparently unconcerned flick of his wrist. After another quick look at his cards, he slid forward on his chair. "Whose bet is it?"

The matter of money dropped for the moment, Dan kept his doubts to himself and concentrated on the game until Chase lost the rest of his stake. The party broke up quickly after that. As the new man, it was his job to sort and store the chips, and he lingered over the task, waiting for a private chat with Bryce. Once the last of the group had departed, the host toted glasses to the bar and asked if he wanted another drink.

Dan held his breath. Here it came, the moment he'd been dreading. Instinct drew him to his full height, but he propped his hands behind him against the card table and forced his body into a relaxed pose. "My plans have changed. I have to withdraw from The Aegean."

Though liquid sloshed against the sides of Bryce's glass, his face remained unperturbed. "What kind of nonsense are you talking?" he asked.

"I'm serious," Dan said. He dropped his chin so he could look Bryce in the eyes. "If you go forward with the project, it'll be without me."

It took another long pull from his glass, but the

development's leader managed to sound blasé when he asked, "Funding problems? I hear you're invested in some community outreach program. You should drop that, stay with us. The poor will always be there. Chances like this don't come around often."

It was Dan's turn to scoff. There had been a time when acceptance by people like Bryce meant the world to him. But no longer. Sensing the situation called for a bold statement, he said, "I'm pulling out. Completely."

"Oh, I get it." Bryce practically sneered as his facade slipped. "I can't say I'm surprised. I took you into the group because Jack insisted, but I always knew a man with your background would never measure up. Too bad. You'd have made a killing."

Dan let the insult roll off.

"Protecting this land from development has become important to me. There are dozens of other locations that would suit your needs. I have a list and, if you want, I'll work with you to find a great spot."

More ice cubes clinked. The level of bourbon in Bryce's bottle dropped another inch.

"Don't bother. We'll find someone to replace you."

"Really?" He had expected Bryce to go ballistic. The man's indifferent attitude raised Dan's suspicion. "Someone like Chase?" he asked.

"Mmph. Maybe. He is one of us, after all. Did I mention that he and his wife have reconciled?"

"The man's a menace," Dan said with slow, careful deliberation. "It's another reason I wanted to speak with you. I took one of his patients back into surgery this afternoon and replaced the mitral valve he supposedly repaired. She would have died otherwise."

No one could do condescension better than the head of the medical society when he put his mind to it.

"You're a heck of a fine surgeon, Dan. We're lucky to have you at the hospital, but that comment only proves my point. Someone with the *right* background would know we never mention another doctor's problems. We fix them." His voice dropped to a guttural undertone. "And if you want to protect your practice, you'll keep our business to yourself."

An hour later, Dan grabbed a soda from his own fridge and stepped out onto the balcony overlooking the ocean. Sometimes, he decided as he sipped straight from the can, being a member of the inner circle wasn't all that it was cracked up to be. Bryce and the development cadre could call it whatever they wanted; at the end of the day, they were still bribing a public official. That potential scandal left him feeling more in need of a shower than he did after a hard workout.

He stood, listening to the waves roll ashore. He'd put a lot on the line by withdrawing from The Aegean group. But at least he'd left the project with his honor intact.

His heart was another matter. He was afraid he'd gone and lost that to Jess and her son. They'd taught him far more than how to catch a fish. And now that he'd torn down the last barrier between them, he intended to go all in and prove to Jess that a forever kind of love was in their cards.

WATCHING DAN'S EASY GAIT as he made his way down the dock, Jess stopped to remind herself that this was not a day when they'd celebrate each catch with a kiss. Not with school on holiday and her son onboard. Still, it couldn't hurt to enjoy the view while her child was busy loading their lunch supplies into the ice chest. In faded jeans and a windbreaker over an On The Fly T-shirt,

Dan couldn't possibly know how sexy he looked. The sight of him warmed her from the inside out.

"Hey, Dr. Hamilton," Adam called sooner than she would have liked. A wide smile broke across the boy's face as he waved.

"Hey, yourself, tiger." Footsteps echoed across the wooden dock until Dan reached the idling boat. "Permission to come aboard, Captain?"

"If that's coffee…" Jess looked into his warm eyes and almost forgot what she was saying. She swallowed and fixed her gaze on the tray he balanced in one hand. "Permission granted."

While she settled their travel mugs and a juice box into cup holders, Dan made the tricky act of stepping down from solid wood onto bobbing fiberglass look as if it was something he'd done all his life, instead of only once before. The boat dipped and swayed as he walked with a sailor's gait across the open deck to her side.

Dan leaned down. "There's something important we need to discuss in private." He tucked a wayward strand of hair behind her ear. "How about coming over to my place this evening?"

Though the brush of his fingers against her cheek sent a shiver through her midsection, she knew they'd have to wait for another night to finish what they'd started in her kitchen.

"I can't. Evy's at her daughter's." Other than when her folks visited, she'd never left her son with anyone but Evy and Sam, who were so close they were practically related.

Adam wedged himself between them. "Do you like PB and J's, Dr. Hamilton? I helped Mom fix them."

Laughter glinted in Dan's dark eyes as he looked

down at the boy. "Depends on the jelly. Strawberry or grape?"

"Grape," said Adam.

Dan chucked the brim of the boy's baseball cap. "When's lunch?" he asked. Turning to face Jess, he said, "Why don't you both come over? I'll fire up the grill. I make a mean burger."

Adam's eyes widened. "Can we, Mom?"

"Sounds good," Jess said, though she was a little confused by the mixed signals. The conversation she'd thought Dan had in mind wasn't fit for five-year-old ears.

"Get settled in now," she said to Adam, "and we'll head out." She poked Dan in the ribs. "You're a surgeon. You took to fly fishing like you were born for it. You spend your spare time helping foster kids. And you cook, too?" She sighed and placed one hand across her heart. "Is there anything you can't do?"

Humor faded from Dan's handsome features. "I haven't been around little kids much. I think I could use some practice in the dad department." Looking as if he'd said more than he'd intended, he crossed to the other side of the boat and took a seat beside Adam. Jess shook her poor, confused head as the two guys commenced a good-natured argument over who would make the biggest catch

After talking it over with her son, she'd reluctantly eased the boat's "no bait" rule. If Adam caught a small fish on a fly line, he could use it for bait. Only, he had to put it on the hook himself. His excitement about the idea had mounted all week. But by midmorning, when he stood on the gently rocking deck with a squirming fish in one hand, a sharp hook in the other, the boy had changed his mind.

He tossed the tiny fish into the water. A move which made them all laugh and eased her fears about the way her son handled peer pressure. The rest of the morning passed quickly. Fish were caught, measured and returned to the river. Lunches were devoured, and almost before she knew it, there was just time for one small detour before they returned to the dock.

A hundred yards out from the power plant that produced much of the county's electricity, Jess throttled back the motor. She bent her knees to accommodate the boat's dip and rise as it rode on two-foot swells. One hand on the wheel, she pointed to a weathered sign.

"Adam, what does that say?"

The little boy ratcheted the zipper halfway down his life vest and back up again. "Go slow 'cause there's manatees." His head tilted to one side. "Do I hav'ta keep wearin' this, Mom?"

"That's the rule." She checked the water behind them, making sure they went slow enough that they left no wake. Boaters who sped through a manatee zone faced stiff fines.

"But why, Mom?"

Busy at the wheel, she was tempted to use the dreaded, "Because I said so," but bit her tongue and said nothing. Without correction, the current and a light wind would drive the twenty-two-foot boat ashore. Keeping it in place demanded her attention.

"I like those fish," Dan intervened from his seat on a storage compartment that doubled as a bench. He pointed to a cluster of particularly colorful figures on Adam's life preserver. "What's that one?"

While Adam stopped to examine his jacket, Dan returned her grateful smile with a fleeting look so full of promise she felt an answering stir of desire. As her heart rate shifted into overdrive, she was sure he'd read her feelings on her face and she ripped her gaze away. Three months ago, she'd been all but certain she'd never fall in love again, yet she no longer questioned the way she felt about Dan. And once more, she wondered how much longer she could keep her love for him a secret.

Adam tugged Dan's sleeve, demanding his attention. The finger he pointed at one of the purple figures on his vest bore traces of peanut butter and jelly. "This one's a manatee."

"Cool," Dan said. "Have you ever seen one?"

"Uh-huh. They're hu-u-ge!" The boy spread his arms as far apart as they could reach. "They eat grass." His little face scrunched with concern. "Not people. Right, Mom?"

"Right," Jess answered without leaving her post behind the wheel. The gentle giants were often called sea cows because they grazed on vegetation along the bottom of the river. She aimed with her chin and cut off the ignition. "And I think one has found us."

Ten feet off the front bow, a smooth patch appeared in a trough between two waves. With a snort and a puff of wind, a wide gray head poked out of the water.

Adam rushed to the side of the boat and stretched out a hand. "C'mere!" he cried.

"No touching," she reminded. Laws prohibited feeding and petting of the endangered species. She took a hasty step toward him as her son leaned out over the rail, intent on getting as close as he could to the seal-like snout.

Dan beat her to it. "Hey, big guy. Watch out there." His hand grasped the straps of Adam's life vest, and Jess's steps slowed.

She'd spent a few sleepless nights fretting over how

well a single man with his background would adapt to the care, feeding and constant need for supervision her five-year-old required. She needn't have worried. If anything, Dan was as protective of Adam as she was. She set the anchor and joined her two favorite guys at the side where they watched a thousand pounds of mottled gray flesh circle the boat until it reached the motor. To Adam's delight, the sea cow scratched his back against the propeller's rounded fins.

Glad that she'd powered down, Jess shook her head. "Not the smartest animal in the kingdom." Nearly every adult had a scar or two from a run-in with a boat.

"Too bad we can't send them all to manatee school. Right, Adam?" Dan leaned down to the boy. His voice took on a cartoonish absurdity. "Lesson number one, class—boats bite."

When Adam laughed as if the joke was the funniest thing he'd ever heard, Jess didn't even try to hide the way her eyes misted. Her son deserved a man in his life. One who came home from work armed for a sock-ball fight and who'd relate to her son in ways that were different—not necessarily better, but different—from Adam's relationship with her. Someone like Dan.

Exactly like Dan.

Her throat tightened as Adam repeated the punch line and broke into fresh gales of laughter. While he marched up and down the length of the boat, periodically shouting, "Boats bite!" Dan slipped an arm around her waist. She leaned against him and stole a quick peek at the man who made her heart melt. Yearning stirred within her when her cheek rubbed against the morning stubble that shadowed his jaw. She longed to run her fingers over its sandpaper roughness. But one look at the pint-size kid rounding the bow and heading in their direction, the one who didn't miss a trick, and she folded her hands. At nearly the same moment, Dan's fingers slipped from her waist.

Manatee, she reminded herself. *Concentrate on the manatee.*

Now was not the time to try and decide whether she and Dan were thinking along the same lines or if she was simply misreading his intentions.

"Can he fish with us again, Mom?" Adam begged after they had waved goodbye to Dan at the dock. "Can he? Okay, Mom? Tomorrow, okay?"

"He has to work, honey," she explained. "And so do I." She held the door while the boy scrambled onto his booster seat and fastened the belt.

"You always have to work." Adam crossed his arms and threw himself back against the upholstery. "I don't want burgers for dinner. I want nuggets 'n' fries. You never take me to the drive-through." Fatigue made his small voice tremble.

A nap would restore his good spirits. That, plus a phone call from Sam and an invitation for Adam to have a sleepover with Sam's grandson changed her expectations for the evening. After promising they could go to Dr. Hamilton's another time, she punched a number she'd programmed into her speed dial. She smiled when Dan answered on the first ring.

"Long time, no hear," he joked.

"Change of plans. Adam's going to spend the night with a friend. You still want company?" She held her breath and waited.

"Even more so. But if it's just the two of us… That menu could stand improvement. You like Champagne? Oysters?" He rattled off a half dozen other choices known for their sensuous qualities.

This time she had no trouble deciphering Dan's intentions. Or deciding if they were on the same track as hers.

They were. They so definitely were that she wondered how she'd make it through the long afternoon.

A store full of customers helped. Before she knew it, her little boy was rested and off to Sam's. And not too much later, she was half listening to the weather forecast while she dabbed on a bit of blush and powder. She was ready to walk out the door when the picture on the television switched from weather maps to a familiar stretch of coastline. The fresh-faced young man on the screen said, "A local property is at center of controversy as the legislative session wraps in Tallahassee. We'll have the complete details for you at eleven o'clock."

Mindless of the wrinkles the move put in her freshly pressed slacks, Jess sank onto the edge of her bed. Had the session ended? Her next question was so critical it made her tummy quiver. Had funding for the cove been approved? Quickly, she reached for her cell and called Bob, confident their man in the capitol would know the score.

When he didn't answer, she left a message asking if he'd been out celebrating or drowning his sorrows. She could scarcely stand the suspense. But no matter which way things went, she knew right where she wanted to be when she heard the news.

The matter of Phelps Cove was up in the air, but Dan's invitation left no room for doubt.

DAN TURNED WHEN THE DOORBELL RANG. He surveyed the apartment one final time. Candles lit. Appetizers on the counter. Woman of his dreams at the door. Check, check and triple check. A quick glance at his reflection in the window of the microwave reassured him that, despite his galloping heart rate, his hair wasn't standing on end. He walked to the door, mentally preparing himself for the night ahead.

Tonight he fully intended to say those three little words. The ones that had never crossed his lips before. But by morning, he planned to say them so often they'd feel familiar in his mouth, though the intensity of his feelings would never fade. Of that, he was certain. He couldn't imagine his life without Jess and Adam in it and tonight he planned to show—and tell—her how he felt.

Wanting to savor the moment, he opened the door wide and stepped back. For a second, he could only stare at the woman who stood in light spilling from his apartment. She'd left her hair down, the soft curls framing her sweet face the way he loved. Her lips were glossy and kissable. A blue top shimmered against her golden skin and cream-colored pants hugged her hips, reminding him of the curves and smooth legs beneath.

"Permission to come aboard, Captain?" she asked.

When her cheery greeting hit a false note, he attributed it to nerves. Which was okay since he had a few of his own. He opened his arms.

"C'mon in," he teased, hoping to put her fears to rest. Folding himself around her smaller figure, Dan breathed kisses into her hair. His senses filled with the citrus fragrance that was as much a part of Jess as her breezy nature. She tipped her head and his mouth closed over her willing lips.

His body responded the way it always did whenever she was within a half mile and he quickly dialed it back a notch. His fingers grazed her soft cheek.

"There's crackers, wine, cheese. Dinner's in the oven. Or we can…"

The decision was hers. Even if the frustration of needing her drove him to summon the men in the white coats rather than live for another moment without her, he would not push.

A wispy tendril had fallen onto her forehead. Searching her face, he brushed it back. The faintest shiver of doubt rushed through him at the look that clouded her dark eyes. He skimmed one hand down her slender arm.

"Everything okay?" he asked.

"Fine," she answered, though clearly, it wasn't.

Her anxious look triggered all his alarms and put his plans for the evening on hold. Time to go to work, he told himself. It was his job to diagnose her problem and excise it. He tested a short list of possibilities while he poured wine and they moved onto the balcony. When questions about Adam and the shop failed to ring any bells, he dug deep, reaching for a scenario that, however unlikely, was still better than the fearful idea that had taken root in his chest.

"This isn't the part where you confess to a torrid love affair with some guy you met on the internet, is it?"

The question brought her head around. "Hardly," Jess answered. The trace of a smile crossed her lips. "Sorry. Guess I'm not very good company." She drew in a breath deep enough to strain the fabric across her breasts. "I caught a blip on the news about Phelps Cove. It sounded like there'd been a development. You don't know what's going on in Tallahassee, do you?"

As a matter of fact, he didn't, and his mouth turned down at the edges, letting his dissatisfaction show. Since his resignation from The Aegean, he hadn't heard so much as a peep from a single member of the invest-ment group. He had no idea if they'd continued with their bribery plan, but he didn't think they'd really be that stupid. The risk was too great, with no guarantee of success.

Not that he could tell Jess about their scheme. As Bryce had made perfectly clear, the medical community frowned on one of its own turning traitor, even when it had nothing to do with medicine. And until things were locked down tight with Estelle Phelps, he didn't dare breathe a word of the meeting he'd arranged with the heiress. So, for the sake of his practice and to preserve Phelps Cove, he had secrets to keep. Even from the woman he loved.

"I have no idea," he lied.

Chapter Thirteen

Jess bit her lower lip as she searched Dan's face. She sensed he wasn't telling her everything he knew, but she resisted the urge to interrogate him. True to his word, Dan had always been honest with her. She wouldn't let fears from the past damage their relationship, or the future she hoped they would share.

Dan cleared his throat. "You want to check the news?"

But Jess had already decided. "You know what," she said before she could change her mind. "I don't want anything to ruin our night. Whatever happens with Phelps Cove, we'll deal with it tomorrow."

With that, she moved into his arms. Her hands twined around his neck and her fingers wove through the lustrous satin of his hair. Her eyes wide-open, she pulled him down until his lips claimed hers exactly the way she'd known they would. *This* was what she wanted, what she'd been waiting for. They kissed until an incredibly sweet pressure grew low in her belly. A soft moan escaped her lips when his fingers slipped beneath the hem of her shirt.

"Want to go inside?" he murmured, his voice a caress against her ear.

Over the flames of desire, she managed a breathless "Yes." She was all about making a beeline for his bedroom. She would have, too, if his pager hadn't beeped at the single most inopportune moment in the history of the world.

His hand automatically reached for the device.

"Don't look. Don't look. Don't look," she mouthed against his neck while reminding herself that she'd chosen to fall in love with a man who couldn't always control his own time.

"My answering service. They wouldn't call unless..."

"Unless it was an emergency." She retreated, her emotions swinging from down from the top arc of the pendulum. "You should call them back."

"I'm not on duty, so this won't take long. Pour us another glass and make yourself at home," he suggested with a kiss full of promise.

Once Dan had disappeared down the hall, Jess returned their glasses to the wine butler. Her quick survey of the living space produced an appreciative whistle. From the magazines stacked at precise angles on an overstuffed ottoman to a jumbo-size television in a designer hutch, everything was neat and tidy. And so unlike her jumbled office at On The Fly, or the kid-friendly home she'd made above the shop, that she battled momentary doubt.

The couch she settled onto wouldn't look so shiny after Adam's first sticky-fingered assault. So how would she and her son and all their mess fit into Dan's life? She leaned back against the soft leather and massaged her forehead.

"One step at a time," she told herself.

She and Dan hadn't even spent a night together, and here she was trying to plan their future. What was she thinking? She was just edgy, keyed up from all Dan's kisses, and worried about Phelps Cove. She needed a distraction. Realizing she'd missed the weather report earlier, she lifted the remote from a hand-carved bowl on the side table.

"State senators and representatives are heading home tomorrow after failing to address any funding issues. The governor expects to call a special session to handle budgetary matters this summer."

Her stomach sank.

Nothing. That's all the legislature had to do in order to ruin Phelps Cove…and it sounded as though they'd done exactly that. How had things gone so wrong? She'd thrown everything she had into the fight for the protected habitat, and she'd still lost. Lost the chance to honor Henry, to preserve the land for future generations.

Defeated, she glanced down the hall where the man she loved had headed. Much as she'd looked forward to *the* night with Dan, the news had robbed her of feeling. She wanted nothing more than to go home, curl up in her bed and sleep until the world became a better place. Or at least until tomorrow. Tears stung her eyes. She wiped them with the backs of her hands.

"In related news, prominent local doctor, Bryce Jones the third, was among a group of people arrested in Tallahassee this afternoon."

Jess fixed a chilly gaze on the screen where police officers led a familiar figure to a cruiser. Her blood turned to ice when the announcer continued.

"Charges are pending, but unnamed sources tell us Dr. Jones is involved in a scheme to bribe members of the state's finance committee. More arrests are expected as investigation into The Aegean development group…"

It didn't take a genius to connect the dots between a bribery scheme and the legislature's funding problems. Faster than she could set a hook, Jess went from cold defeat to white-hot anger. The shove she gave the remote sent it skidding across the leather ottoman where it toppled the stack of magazines. The commotion was loud enough to draw Dan's attention. He caught up with her on the way to the door.

"Something break?" He sent a troubled frown over her shoulder to the living room.

"Just my heart," Jess shot back. She jabbed a finger toward the television where Bryce, along with several others, were being loaded into police cars. The way Dan's face fell when he saw the screen only confirmed her fears. She let her voice rise on an angry tide. "Bribery, Dan?"

"Now, Jess, it's not what it looks like," he protested.

"It looks pretty clear to me. Or are you trying to tell me that's not one of your pals they're hauling off to jail? Did you know about this?"

"Not about the arrests. No."

But he knew something. Guilt was all over his face. Swinging her head to one side, she held up a hand. "But you knew about the bribes. And you didn't tell me?"

He looked so vulnerable standing there that if she hadn't seen the images herself, heard the reporter herself, she might have given him a second chance. As much as it hurt, though, she couldn't ignore the truth. It was just her luck that the one time she'd opened her heart since Tom died, the man she'd trusted it with had shattered her dreams.

"I thought I could trust you. That you'd be honest with me. But this?" Her voice had developed a wounded quality that made her even angrier. "You were just using me to get what you wanted." Her thoughts were coming so fast and furious she paused to let her mouth catch up.

"Well," she huffed. "You can forget about George's help once he hears about this. Or was Connections House another one of your scams?"

And if it was, what would people say about her involvement? Would they recognize her as the victim? Or would they accuse her of being part of the conspiracy?

The thought made her chest hurt.

"Jess, slow down. You'll see it's not what you're thinking."

She'd always supposed Dan's ability to remain calm in an emergency made him a better doctor. It did not serve him well in a fight.

She overrode his even tone. "You know, this is the same kind of stuff Tom used to pull. He never told me about all the risks he was taking, the same way you neglected to mention that your pals were spreading money all over Tallahassee. There isn't any difference, Dan. Tom lied, and so did you."

"You're wrong, Jess," Dan began in the same soothing voice. "I didn't tell you everything, but I didn't lie to you."

"Oh, really? You can't deny that you left out a few important facts." He'd hurt her. She needed to wipe that smug look off his face and make him feel the same pain. "I'm thinking that bribery is a pretty underhanded way to get what you want. I'm thinking that a man who would resort to it would do just about anything. And I'm thinking the police might be knocking on his door next."

And how would that look, if she were there when they showed up? The one spearheading the Phelps Cove campaign caught in bed—despite herself, she groaned—with the opposition. How would she explain to Adam that his mommy had had the bad sense to get involved with a man who couldn't be trusted? And who would take care of her boy until she proved her innocence?

Acid rose in the back of her throat as somewhere within her a dam burst and her worst fears for her child's future poured out.

"Jess, please listen—"

"What kind of man are you to use me like this?" She had to get out of there. She had to do it right now. She pushed aside the hand Dan reached to her. "Don't even try to defend yourself. You lied. About this and who knows what else. I should have known better than to let myself fall for someone like you, someone with no ties to anything."

She meant nothing to tie him to the land, but the way Dan's color deepened told her he'd taken the cut much more personally. For the first time, she heard anger in his voice.

"So, after all your talk, pedigree matters to you?"

"Of course not," she protested. An ache started in her heels and worked its way up into her head. "I can't… I can't… I don't know what to believe anymore."

"Well, you're wrong about me, Jess, but that makes two of us because I was wrong about you, too. I thought you were the kind of woman who'd love me for who I am. Not someone who'd hold where I came from against me."

Pain and anger warred, sending her voice higher. "All I know is, I can't deal with this, with you, right now. I'm out of here."

While Dan remained a silent presence, she snatched her purse from the entryway table and marched to the parking lot. Once behind the wheel of her car, she pressed her hand against her chest to keep her heart from shattering into a million pieces. Somehow, she managed to hold it together long enough to make it home.

By midnight, she'd exhausted all her tears and climbed into bed. But a broken heart made a poor bed-fellow, so she turned the television to a channel that advertised all local news, all the time. In between repeated broadcasts, she passed the long, sleepless night reliving the breakup. By two, she'd watched the same footage so often it looked as tired as she felt. She brewed a pot of coffee at three and sat at the kitchen table until the sky along the eastern horizon lightened from black to gray.

By then, she'd been over the scene with Dan enough times to suspect she'd let her mouth get ahead of her heart and ruined everything.

Sure, Dan was to blame for getting involved with The Aegean group, but she'd been wrong, too. Wrong to fire accusations without giving him a chance to explain. Wrong not to realize there had to be more to the story. Not only that, but she'd thrown the absolute worst insult imaginable his way. She'd damaged their relationship beyond repair.

A lifetime might pass before she let someone get that close again, but Dan had loved her. Now that she was thinking clearly, she knew he had. Hadn't he proven it in a thousand small ways? She thought of stolen kisses, how his hand always seemed to find hers, the late-night phone calls after exhausting surgeries, the attention he showered on her son.

But the man who had loved her had also betrayed

her. And the worst part was that they'd never get back what they'd tossed away. She clamped her hand over her mouth as another piece of her heart broke and fresh tears began to fall.

DAN GRABBED HIS PILLOW and pulled it tight around his head. No good. The incessant beeping would not be ignored.

He was five stories up. How could the garbage trucks sound so loud?

A quick check of his bedside clock revealed only a blur. He pried open his eyes and blinked until the numbers swam into focus. A groan escaped his lips. He hadn't slept till nine in over a decade. Of course, he hadn't polished off a bottle of wine on his lonesome or been dumped by the love of his life in the past ten years, either.

How had things gotten to this point?

A week ago, the dream of a home for foster kids had been within his grasp. And last night, with the woman he loved in his arms, he'd seen a quaint four-bedroom in his own future. A place with a fenced yard out back and a boat dock in the front. A family kind of house. The kind Adam, and maybe a sister or a brother—or two—would call home.

Now, he'd lost both Jess and Adam. And maybe even more than that.

Propping an arm behind his head, he told himself that he was an old hand at the pain of rejection. It was his destiny and, by now, he should have been used to it.

Jess had never even heard his side of the story, but it didn't matter. One thing he knew about her, once she made up her mind, she didn't change it. As wrong as she was about him, though, she'd been dead right about one thing. Connections House would never survive if he remained a part of it. Even if his association with The Aegean group had ended well before Bryce's trip to Tallahassee, the scent of scandal still clung to him. One whiff and George and his pals would pull their support. He had no choice; he had to step away and hope they'd follow through on their commitments.

Another round of beeping began. Fully awake this time, he recognized the difference between a truck backing up and the sound of the pager on his bedside table. With another groan, he threw back the covers and stumbled into his jeans.

In the kitchen, he grabbed a bottle of aspirin and downed three pills with a large glass of water. As his brain caught up with the rest of him, he braced his hands on the granite counter. A quick call to his answering service alerted him that the hospital board had scheduled an emergency meeting, and his presence was required. Evidently, the powers-that-be had been less than pleased to wake up to the news that several of their own were now facing felony charges. Careers were on the line, and Dan didn't need to hear the words to know his was one of them.

After promising to be there in an hour, he poured an extra scoop of grounds into the coffeepot and started the brew cycle. A shower and a shave were in order, as well. But before that, he needed to gather the faxes and paperwork to prove he'd broken his association with The Aegean group long before the Tallahassee debacle. Otherwise, he might be out of a job. And the way his life was going, it was the only thing he had left.

That, and one last fishing lesson with Jess.

Hope bloomed at the thought. Could he get her back?

He filled a mug and took a swig of coffee that was far too bitter.

Not a chance.

He'd seen the hurt and despair in her eyes when she left. Her love for him had died. And with it, he'd lost all hope of having a family to call his own.

JESS MIGHT HAVE STAYED in bed for a month if she hadn't had a business to run and a son to raise. Customers came and went despite her broken heart. Supply lists had to be filled whether her tears dripped on them or not. Employees noted her sad mood and treated her with kid gloves, but still wanted their paychecks. And little boys required food and comfort and care. Especially one whose newest, bestest friend had disappeared and who sensed that, somehow, Mom was to blame.

It took a week before she drew a full breath without cringing. Even then, it was too soon to see Dan again. One look at the broad chest where she'd never again be welcome to lay her head, a peek into the brown eyes that would no longer light up whenever they saw her, and her fragile heart would shatter all over again. Knowing she might never patch herself back together if that happened, she motioned Sam into her office on Tuesday, shortly before On The Fly closed.

"You know Dan and I aren't seeing each other any-more." Her chest burned when she said his name. She cleared her throat. "We're not actually on speaking terms."

"The way you've been mopin' around the last few

days, I sort of figured that out." Sam leaned forward. "Adam okay?"

"He's finally stopped asking about Dan every ten minutes. He'll be all right." If she'd learned anything from the experience, it was that next time she'd keep her love life away from her son.

Not that there would likely be a next time.

"No chance you'll get back together? I thought you two were good for each other, Jess."

"No." Wishing the truth didn't hurt quite so much, she pressed one hand to her chest. "I accused him of using me to get Phelps Cove."

"He did what?" To his credit, Sam was instantly on her side. He sprang to his feet. "Let me at him, Jess. I'll teach the..."

She waved her hand, cutting him off. "I should have known from the beginning we'd never work things out. I had too much riding on Phelps Cove. When the legislature didn't approve the money for it, I... Well, neither of us likes to lose. I said some awful things. Unforgiveable things."

"Seems to me, the doc ain't no saint. Haven't his partners been accused of bribery?"

"Yeah." But none of the reporters had mentioned Dan's name. She'd followed all the coverage during a week of sleepless nights that seemed to stretch out forever.

"The bottom line is, no matter what he's done or hasn't done, he's still a valued client and we need to treat him like one."

Disbelief showed on the manager's weathered face. "Whoa, that's a switch."

"It is, isn't it?" She shook her head at the irony. Thanks to Dan's advice, her attitude toward their customers had improved and along with it, the shop's bottom line.

"All right." Sam gave a resigned sigh and returned to his chair. "What can I do?"

"I need you to handle his last fly fishing lesson."

"Sure you wouldn't rather I toss him overboard?" Sam asked. "Somewhere near the middle of the river?"

"I'm sure," she said, working up a small smile. "Word might get around."

They mapped out a plan to fish off one of the spoil islands where trout always bit. When they were done, she looked up from the spot she'd circled on the chart to find Sam studying her face.

"You sure you can't make things right? He's always struck me as a man you could reason with."

"Trust me on this," Jess said, echoing the words she'd heard Dan use. She'd hurt him as much as he'd hurt her. There was no going back. Once Sam gave Dan this final lesson, it would sever the last of her ties to him. She'd be free to move on, if she could. "It's over between us."

"You're the boss." Sam sighed heavily. He rolled the chart and slid it into a waterproof tube. "I don't mean to add to your troubles, but you did hear he walked away from Connections House, didn't you?"

It was news to her, though the move made sense. George and his friends hadn't acquired their considerable clout by associating with criminals. Rather than see his dream suffer through guilt by association, Dan had let it go, placing it in other hands for safekeeping. Which did nothing for her goal of falling out of love with the man. She checked her watch. She was going to need a new timetable for getting over him.

With the map under one arm, Sam edged toward the door. "Okay if I call the doc now?"

No, it wasn't okay, but she whispered, "Go ahead."

Business was, after all, business. And without Phelps Cove to protect or Dan to love, she'd do what had to be done to keep On The Fly in the black and to raise her son to be an honest man.

THE NEXT MORNING, SHE ANSWERED the phone at On The Fly with her standard greeting.

"It's about time I caught you," Bob said. "I've been trying to reach you all week."

The head of POE sounded far too upbeat for a man who'd had two years' worth of work ripped out from under him. Of course, his ties to the organization went a lot deeper than one piece of property. Bob'd probably already lined up a replacement for Phelps Cove and was calling to enlist her help in securing it. If so, she hated to be the one to break it to him, but she didn't have enough fight left in her to lose again.

"Are you sitting down?" he asked. Before she had a chance to remind him he'd called her at work, Bob continued, "Estelle Phelps has given us an extension on the contract for Phelps Cove. Is that fantastic or what?"

The words blew a hole in the fog of pain that had enveloped her ever since the breakup. Her mouth dropped open, but no sound came out. Trying to pull her thoughts together, she could only manage, "What? How?" before numb shock shut her down again.

"Look, POE wants to move fast on this. A couple of weeks, tops. I've spoken with our lawyers and they're already finalizing the paperwork."

"But how? We still don't have the money. The legislature—"

"Where have you been this last week? On Mars? You haven't heard the news?"

"I've been a little, um, under the weather." She was pretty sure that didn't count as a lie. Broken hearts had a lot in common with the flu, and every time she thought of Dan, she felt nauseous.

"So you don't know what's going on in Tallahassee," Bob said. "I haven't seen this much turmoil in years."

"Give me the condensed version," she suggested.

"You got it. The governor is up in arms about the budget. He's hauling the legislature back into session next week. And now that Estelle Phelps has removed her objections, the purchase of Phelps Cove will sail through."

"You can't be serious." Jess went so weak in the knees she leaned against the counter.

"No lie," Bob answered cheerily. "Look, I didn't want to say anything until we were certain, but Phelps Cove is going to need a full-time manager. Someone to oversee construction of the visitor's center and guide our efforts to protect the habitat. Think about it, Jess. You'd be perfect for the job. I gotta run, but I'll get back in touch soon."

"Yeah, sure, Bob. Thanks for letting me know."

Slowly she lowered the phone into the cradle. She'd never imagined success would taste so bittersweet. She'd achieved everything she'd set out to do. Adam was growing into a bright, articulate child. Sales were up at On The Fly. And not only were the two years she'd devoted to Phelps Cove finally paying off, but the perfect job was hers for the asking.

So, why couldn't she summon up enough emotion for one lousy "yippee"?

Chapter Fourteen

Jess locked down the zipper on the slim skirt of her best black suit and checked her image in the mirror. The subdued and professional look she wore to camouflage her broken heart stared back. She added a dusting of blush over her wan cheeks, a shimmer of gloss to her pale lips. Wispy curls escaped her businesslike French twist, but at least the circles under her eyes had faded. She had the recent increase in sales at On The Fly to thank for a string of long days with no time for might-have-beens. But fatigue hadn't kept her from dreaming of a certain dark-haired man who had swept her off her feet. She knew her dreams would fade…eventually. She'd give it a year.

Or maybe ten.

She noted the time and slid her feet into the kick-ass heels that gave her morale the boost she needed. Holding a civil conversation with Henry's niece had been a challenge from day one and, despite the woman's recent change of heart, Jess didn't trust her. If Estelle pulled a last-minute trick at today's ceremony, she'd have a fight on her hands.

"Gotta love the cool, calm and collected new you,"

Jess told her reflection. When her laugh fell flat, she drew in a steadying breath. "Ready, Adam?" she called.

"Yep. Is this okay?"

Her boy, who was growing up far too quickly, skidded into the room. His comb had left wavy teeth marks in wet, slicked-back hair. Water dribbled past his ears and trailed down his cheeks. His shirt was half-tucked, and she'd bet the socks beneath his Sunday pants didn't match.

For Adam's sake, she mustered up a smile. "Perfect. And me? How do I look?"

Her quick spin failed to impress the going-on-six-year-old. He leaned back, arms folded across his chest.

"Those shoes are too tall," he said with all the solemnity of a judge.

"That's why they call them *high* heels." Balancing on one foot, she danced the other through the air. "I like them. They make me feel pretty." Something she hadn't felt since the last time she'd seen herself mirrored in Dan's eyes. But thinking about their lost love would only lead to tears and she'd sworn today's events would seal her heartache in the past.

There'd be no looking back.

Despite Bob's assurances that everything would turn out well, a series of minor snafus had delayed the transfer of Phelps Cove for six long weeks. At last, the big day had arrived, and, with it, her determination to move forward. She'd do it the way she'd done everything else since that fateful night when she'd let her mouth get ahead of her heart. She'd do it by focusing on the details.

"Is your bag by the door?"

"Yes, ma'am."

"Do you have enough books and toys?"

"I could prob'ly use more cars." Adam's mouth slanted to one side.

"Better get them," she advised. "We're out of here in two minutes, and you won't be able to talk to me during the meeting."

On the way there, she searched her heart for the giddy joy she'd always imagined at this moment. Instead, she found the same low calm that lay across the river on either side of the causeway to the mainland. The glassy surface of the water made a perfect day for fly fishing, and she knew without checking the forecast that reds were feeding on crabs in Phelps Cove.

Six weeks ago, she would have called Dan on a day like this. If he was free, she'd take him out on the boat to hunt for reds. But those days were over. She told herself it was time to get used to her new reality, the one that didn't include the hunky doctor.

Within minutes, her heels tapped against the marble floors of an old bank building in downtown Cocoa. Adam skidded to a dead stop beneath the lobby's vaulted ceilings.

"Whoo-whooo," he said tentatively. Echoes bounced around him and his eyes grew wide. Louder, he said, "Whoo-whoo-oo."

"Shh," Jess cautioned. "Not now." If things went well enough upstairs, they'd both have something to shout about after the meeting. She crossed her fingers and hoped for the best.

Once Adam was playing contentedly under the secretary's watchful eyes, Jess hurried to the conference room. There, everyone who had anything to do with Phelps Cove held their breath while Estelle completed her portion of the paperwork. A round of handshakes polished off the anticlimactic transfer of assets and, soon after, people began slipping out the door. The group dwindled down until only Jess and Estelle lingered over coffee.

"Congratulations," Jess offered while they waited for copies of the signed contracts. "Henry would be proud of what you did here today."

Estelle's smile barely reached her eyes. "I'm happy enough with the way things turned out. And you? I hear they've put you in charge."

"The job is a dream come true," she admitted. Sam had jumped at the chance to run On The Fly. With that settled, she'd accepted Bob's offer. Volunteers and construction crews would be busy for a year restoring the riverside to a pristine wilderness and erecting the necessary facilities. After that, she had plans for an eco-center where school kids would learn how to protect their environment. "The offer to name the sanctuary after you still stands."

"No thanks," Estelle answered. She helped herself to more coffee. "The Henry Phelps Center has a nice ring to it."

Jess supposed that two and a half million dollars gave one the right to be magnanimous. But now that the papers had been signed and there was no backing out, her curiosity surfaced.

"What changed your mind?" she asked. "The Aegean's offer fell apart, but you could have held out for a better price. Sooner or later, you'd have gotten it."

A sigh worthy of a New York stage passed through Estelle's lips, and her hair fell forward. She tucked it behind one ear. "It was never about the money. It was about my children. I wanted to ensure their future."

She rolled one ultra-thin shoulder. "Seeing a man like Bryce Jones arrested gave me second thoughts. It made me think that setting a better example might be the best thing I could do for them." She blew a cooling breath across her beverage and took a sip. "It *is* what Uncle Henry wanted. And who knows? Maybe he'll put in a good word with the man upstairs and I'll get a star in my crown."

She paused and her smile turned crafty. "That young doctor friend of yours seemed to think so."

Fine china rattled as Jess lost her grip on the handle of her cup.

"Oh. Wasn't I supposed to mention that?" Estelle snapped her perfectly manicured fingers. "That's right. He asked me not to. But a guy who would go so far out on a limb for a gal deserves a little credit, doesn't he?"

"Dan." Jess flattened her palms against the table so her fingers would stop shaking. There wasn't anything she could do to mask the way her voice trembled. "Dan Hamilton called you?"

"He did more than call," Estelle said with a marginal lift of one eyebrow. "Remember that escrow account I asked you to fund? He offered to do it for you. Of course, it wasn't necessary. I'd already made my decision by then. But it was a nice gesture."

One tiny sprig of hope poked through the shriveled husk of Jess's heart. "And when, exactly, did this take place?" Before the breakup made it the nice gesture Estelle thought it was. After meant there was a chance he still loved her.

"Let me check my calendar."

While the other woman rummaged in a bag that probably cost more than Jess's checking-account balance, her heart began to race. She chewed on her lower lip while the heiress flipped the pages of a gilt-edged notebook.

"Let's see." Estelle pointed to a date. "He and I met two weeks after all The Aegean mess hit the news." With a coy look, she asked, "Does that help?"

Jess gripped the table to ward off sudden vertigo. When her head cleared, she searched Estelle's sharp features. She had never known Henry's niece to show one hint of embarrassment. Yet, the face across the table took on the faintest pink tinge.

"Well," Estelle announced. "I think I've exhausted my daily quota of good deeds." Standing, she transformed from nearly human into her old self. "If you'll excuse me, I must be going. Be a dear and have them mail everything to me, won't you?"

The world took on a dreamlike quality as Estelle left without the paperwork she'd declared too important to relegate to a courier. Jess remained where she was, her head in her hands, her thoughts a jumbled mess. She looked up as Adam rushed in.

"Mama, the lady at the desk says it's lunchtime." He slid to a halt in front of her. His head tilted. In a voice filled with wonder, he asked, "Are you crying?"

She quickly wiped her eyes with the backs of her hands.

"No, honey," she answered. Not anymore. But if her son suspected tears, she hadn't kept her emotions in check as well as she'd given herself credit for. She'd do a better job, she promised, right after she cleared the air with the handsome doctor who might, just might, still be in love with her.

"That lady gave me donuts," Adam said. "She said they'd tied me up, but they didn't."

Jess clamped a hand over a laugh that bordered on

hysteria. "Tide me over," she corrected. "She meant you wouldn't be hungry for a while." Platters of donuts had gone practically untouched by the people who'd gathered for the closing. She'd told the secretary Adam could have one. "How many?" she asked with sudden suspicion.

"Three," he answered, holding up stubby fingers.

"Yeah, no lunch for you for a while. Let's get your stuff and head downstairs. You can shout in the big room like I promised."

She might even join in. A couple of rebel yells in the lobby would let off some steam and serve as a warm-up for the words she intended to say as soon as she saw Dan.

DAN SCRIBBLED NOTES in the thick folder of diagnostic reports he'd been studying for the past twenty minutes and shoved it to one side. The surgery next week was routine. A good thing because, ever since the night Jess had left, even his morning shave taxed his concentration skills.

He drummed his pen against the desk, wondering how long he could go on this way. He'd been certain he could wait Jess out, that she'd eventually come to her senses. That was before the hours had stretched into days, the days into a week. Even then, he'd thought they had a chance...until she'd sent Sam to teach his last fly fishing lesson. After that, he'd accepted the obvious—she'd fallen out of love with him, and he had only himself to blame.

The door to his office burst open, and he swung away from the window. His pen clattered to the desk top.

As if his thoughts had summoned her, an irate Jess Cofer marched into his office, a woman on a mission.

She stood with one hand propped on a slim hip, and there was no mistaking her fiery temper. Or the chorus of *hallelujahs* that played in his head when she practically shouted, "What were you thinking, letting me walk away from you like that?"

If that wasn't an invitation to make things right between them, he didn't know what was.

But his gut clenched when he took one glance at the little boy who clung to Jess's side with a thumb in his mouth. Adam's insecurity raised the ante in a game where everything was already at stake and made Dan fume. He'd been mourning the breakup so much he hadn't stopped to consider how it affected the boy he'd grown to love.

"Hold on a sec." He directed the comment to Jess.

In his bottom drawer rested a video he'd purchased for Adam when he thought they'd be spending a lot more time together as a family. He took it out, saying, "Hey, tiger. There's a TV in the corner there. Want to watch while Mom and I talk?" He held up the latest G-rated release.

"Okay." Adam scuffed one foot against the carpet, a move so much like his mom's that Dan blinked his eyes to clear them.

"Now, what's all this about?" he asked, once the boy was so engrossed in the show that a herd of ponies could have stormed through the room without breaking his attention. Not taking any chances, he stood between them, his body a shield against curious young eyes.

Jess scrubbed her hands on her skirt. The way she bit her lip told him she was so nervous that if her hair hadn't been pulled back in some elaborate do, her fingers would be twisting through her curls. Wanting to get past this part, he spoke first.

"I lied to you. You know that, don't you?"

Sure, his intentions had been good. And his lies had been more omissions than out-and-out falsehoods. But knowing how much she loathed deceit, he also knew this was their biggest stumbling block.

"You did." She sighed. "You did that."

"And I shouldn't have. I'm sorry." He waited, afraid to move, almost afraid to breathe. If she forgave him now, they'd find a way back to each other. If she didn't, it was over.

Her weight shifted atop impossibly tall heels. Instead of accepting his apology, she said, "You knew I wasn't being fair. You should have stopped me."

Dan propped one arm against the window a safe distance from the woman he'd loved and lost, and, heaven help him, wanted to love for the next fifty or sixty years. He couldn't, however, shoulder all the blame for their breakup. She'd had a part in it, too.

"I tried," he said simply. "You wouldn't let me get a word out. You saw the news and you concluded…"

Jess's eyes widened. Her hands unfurled.

"Jumped," she corrected. "Go ahead and say it. I know you're dying to." A glimmer of a smile crossed her lips. "You think I jumped to a conclusion."

"Okay, you jumped." He couldn't help smiling back at her. Banter had always been a part of their relationship, but they hadn't resolved anything. He sobered quickly. "I thought you knew me better than that."

By now, she had to realize that he wasn't involved in the bribery scheme. He had tried to tell her. He'd tried to warn the group, too, for all the good it did.

"I did. I do know better." She ran her hand over the lips he wanted to kiss. "And I'm sorry, too. I was so confused that night. I thought we'd lost Phelps Cove. Then, when I saw that whole mess with The Aegean…"

She drew herself nearly tall enough to look him straight in the eye. The movement flexed the muscles beneath her skirt, reminding him of how drawn to her he'd been the day he first saw her in Phelps Cove.

"I was wrong."

Jess might be a little quick to draw and fire, it might take her a while to reconsider, but she'd never been afraid to admit when she made a mistake. He loved that about her, but it was only one of many things that made her special.

"When did you figure it out?" The pain she'd felt at the false betrayal echoed within him.

Jess slumped. "When Estelle told me you offered to back our bid for Phelps Cove."

Dan eased up as he realized Jess's golden tan had faded to a winter pallor. The past few weeks had been as hard on her as they had on him. "The money I'd planned to invest was just sitting there. Connections House was funded, thanks to you. Putting the money in an escrow account seemed like a reasonable thing to do."

"That's a mighty big favor. Not the kind of thing you'd do for just anyone."

They'd been dancing around the truth long enough. It was time to come clean.

"I didn't do it for just anyone, Jess. I did it because I love you. Your hopes, your dreams are important to me. If I could help you protect Phelps Cove, I wanted to do it."

"What?" she asked. "What did you just say?" Confusion and hope filled her dark eyes.

He closed the distance between them, cupping her elbows in his, and said the words he'd longed to say.

"I said, I love you, Jessica Cofer. There will never be another woman for me. I've wanted you since the first moment I saw you fishing in Phelps Cove."

The stunned silence that greeted his confession lasted so long, Dan's worst fear resurfaced. Had he been wrong about them? Quieting his doubts, he slipped a finger under Jess's chin and lifted.

"This is the place where you say you love me, too," he said. And waited. He lost a year of his life in the time it took her slow smile to spread across her lips.

"Oh, I do. I love you, Dan. I wanted to tell you, but I thought I'd ruined it between us. I thought you'd fallen out of love with me. I never dreamed…"

"That time, you did jump to a conclusion. The wrong one," he pointed out. Not that he'd done any better. He'd assumed he'd lost her forever.

"Enough talking," he grumbled.

One by one, he took the pins from her hair. The curls he loved cascaded down to her shoulders.

He bent low, knowing that, with Adam in the room, they'd have to save the best for later. Gently, he explored her lips, wanting more but unwilling to assert any claim until she entwined her arms about his neck and pulled him close. When she swept her tongue along his teeth, his blood headed south so fast it took all logic and thought with it. A possessive groan rose in his chest as he trailed kisses along her chin, and down to the soft hollow at the base of her throat. A hint of spicy citrus filled his senses and he breathed it in, letting his lungs expand with the scent that was hers alone. He couldn't get enough of her and traced the outline of her jaw with one thumb.

"Is it lunchtime yet?" came a quiet voice from the end of the room.

Reluctantly, Dan broke the kiss with Jess and traced one finger over a ruby lip.

"Rain check?" he murmured.

A breathless "Oh, yeah," let him know he'd be redeeming that claim ticket before another night passed. Turning, he slipped an arm around her waist and pulled her close.

"Okay, lunchtime," he agreed. "Adam, what'll it be— nuggets 'n' fries?"

As if he sensed the change in the atmosphere, the little boy's gaze traveled from one adult to the other. His solemn look settled on Dan.

"Is that what you're having?" he asked.

Dan shook his head. "Nope. I'm a burger man."

A broad grin split Adam's little face and the mirth that twinkled in his eyes made Dan's heart skip a beat. "Then, I'm a burger man, too," he claimed.

Chapter Fifteen

Dan drove past the sign welcoming visitors to the future home of the Henry Phelps Protected Habitat. The fence surrounding the property was so new, spiders hadn't nested in the chain link but—leave it to Jess—a list of rules already hung beside the gate. They were simple and boiled down to "Don't leave anything behind," and "Don't take anything with you," the two principles she had drilled into his head during their initial fly fishing lessons.

A lot had changed in the six months since his first visit to the cove. On either side of the road—which boasted a fresh layer of gravel—the efforts of POE volunteers were obvious. Leaves on the orange trees had turned glossy and dark green. With proper care, they'd serve as a testament to the area's early settlers. He'd been part of the demolition team that had broken down the old caretaker's cottage, board by weathered board. The salvaged lumber was slated for the Tom Cofer Overlook at the top of the bluff. Survey sticks outlined the site for the Visitors' Center where construction would start tomorrow. After that, workmen would swarm the area, so today was his last chance.

Was he ready?

One glimpse of the woman in the clearing ahead, and he wondered what had taken him so long. In Jess's arms, he'd learned the true meaning of security. In her dark eyes, he'd found all the love and acceptance he'd ever need, and so much more. Recently, he'd put a deposit on their riverside dream house, a place he hoped would be their home for the rest of their lives. Call him old-fashioned, but before Adam and Jess moved in, he wanted to slip a ring on her finger and to promise her forever.

He glanced at the picnic basket on the seat beside him. Nestled within was a tiny box, one that did not hold a diamond. He brushed aside a last-minute whisper of uncertainty. Yes, he could have splurged on the biggest, gaudiest bauble available, but he had to trust that he'd made the right choice.

Assuming Jess gave the answers he wanted to hear to two of the hardest questions he'd ever have to ask.

He parked the car in the shade and swallowed his unease while, hand-in-hand, mother and son hustled toward him pointing and wearing the smiles he wanted to see forever.

"Isn't this a nice surprise," Jess said with a glance at the interior of the brand-new SUV. She leaned in through the window and kissed him, light and easy, out of deference to Adam who had yanked open the passenger door and was busy counting the cup holders and eyeing the DVD player.

"It was time to trade the Beamer in for a larger model. This one's a hybrid. Gets great gas mileage." To say nothing of the cargo space, which was big enough to hold a team's worth of baseball, football or soccer equipment.

"That's a nice surprise, too," she teased, "but I meant,

can an important man like you afford to take time off in the middle of the day?" If Dan wasn't working in his office, he usually spent lunch hours at Connections House.

"I'm the boss." Dan pretended to tuck his thumbs beneath nonexistent suspenders. "I make my own schedule." He'd been relieved when the hospital board hadn't held his former association with The Aegean group against him. Especially when the sudden exposure of illegal dealings had led to a slew of "early retirements" and created such a vacuum that he'd been appointed the new head of the medical society.

"This is a cool car," Adam pronounced. "But why does it smell like chicken?"

"Didn't you know?" Dan patted the dash. "There's a flock of them in the engine compartment."

Adam shot a quick glance at the hood and back again. "No, there isn't," he challenged.

Rather than answer, Dan hefted a picnic basket. "I have enough right here to feed a small army." He wiggled his eyebrows. "Maddy made it." The boy had eaten two helpings at Connections House the past Sunday and pronounced hers the best ever.

"Is it lunchtime yet?" Clutching his stomach, Adam doubled over. "I'm star-r-rving."

Dan ruffled the kid's hair. "Almost." He popped the lid on the trunk. "Why don't you get our fly rods out of the back."

While the boy scurried around to the rear of the car, Dan stepped out and pulled Jess close. "I thought I'd help out by bringing lunch. What do you say we eat down by the water?"

Jess's sunshiny face peered up at his. "A surprise visit, and you brought food? I have to agree with Adam,

I'm starving. Just give me ten or fifteen minutes to finish something up, and I'll meet you there."

He leaned down and planted a kiss atop her head. "Take your time," he suggested, knowing he'd wait for her forever if he had to. He threw a look over his shoulder at Adam. "Let's get out of your mom's hair, okay?"

"Can I have a leg first? What else is in there?"

Dan swung the picnic basket high and out of reach of the kid who, he swore, had grown two inches since dinner last night. "You'll have to wait for your mom. Okay?"

Grumbling good-naturedly, Adam joined him, and they made their way down a path through the woods to the water's edge. There, the table and chairs Dan had toted to the secluded spot the day before sat beneath massive oak trees. He dusted things off, unfurled a table-cloth and tucked the small box in his pocket while he went over his plans one last time.

Jess would sit *there*. Adam would sit *there*. He'd kneel *there*.

His preparations complete, he turned to the boy who'd plunked himself in one of the chairs and stared at the picnic basket with eyes that could test the firmest resolve.

"What say we get our lines wet while we wait..." He was going to explain that it made no sense to tempt the area's critters by opening the food containers, but his words trailed off with one look at the river. "Adam, have you ever seen that before?"

Twenty yards from shore, the river churned with splashing fish. Black-spotted tails wiggled above the water line. Here and there, a golden fin cut through the surface.

"Reds," Adam whispered reverently.

"Let's get 'em," Dan whispered back. The elusive quarry remained at the top of his must-catch list.

They practically tiptoed to the water's edge where Dan bowed to Adam and let the boy take the first cast.

Nada.

While the child stripped line and prepared to try again, Dan tossed his fly near the seething school. A firm tug rewarded his first attempt. The thought that he had a red on the line had barely registered when he looked over and saw that Adam's second cast had paid off handsomely.

Not even nearly-six-year-olds who'd been fishing all their lives were up to the challenge of landing a mature red, and the boy was already struggling. He'd planted his feet firmly in the sand, but the fish was so strong, it had pulled his rod tip down nearly to the ground. His reel chattered as the fish headed for the safety of open water. Without a doubt, the kid was going to lose it.

There really was no choice.

Dan gave a sharp downward tug on his line, pulling the barbless hook free of a red mouth and quickly reeled in. Shedding equipment, he moved to help the boy. One hand on Adam's belt—lest the kid follow the fish into the river—and one hand on the rod, they fought together.

Line keened and peeled along a path as straight as a laser. One hundred feet and the red had taken all of Adam's fly line. Reels were loaded for situations exactly like this, and the green cord changed to white backing before the red settled down. As the fish rested, the thick filament went slack, dipping and drifting toward the water's surface.

"Now, Adam," Dan coached the way Jess had taught him.

Small hands blurred into action. Seaweed hung from the line Adam lifted from the water. It sloughed off as he recovered half the distance before the fish realized it was still hooked.

"Aw, man," he exclaimed when the fish ran again. "I can't..."

"Stay with him. Let him tire himself out. Reel in whenever there's slack."

The boy was a good listener. He leaned forward, letting the red have its way. The second run was shorter. A third, shorter still. After each, he waited only until the line quit singing before he reeled and coaxed and did it again.

In a matter of minutes, two feet of coppery fins and scales splashed in shallow water at Adam's feet. By then, Jess was there, camera in hand. She insisted Dan pose for a photo with the wildly grinning boy and his two-foot "monster."

"How much did you see?" he asked her once they'd returned the fish to the river. Adam raced along the shoreline, proclaiming his victory to every bird and rock within earshot.

"You mean, did I see you let your fish go?"

Love glowed in her eyes when they met his.

So much for the best-laid plans, Dan thought. There'd never be another moment as right as this one.

Tugging the small box from his pocket with hands that trembled so much he could barely flip the lid open, he dropped to one knee. "Jess," he began. Emotion clogged his throat. He cleared it and started over.

"Jess, I'd be the luckiest man on earth if you'd do me the honor of becoming my wife."

A thousand-pound weight dropped from his chest when she whispered, "Yes, oh, yes!"

She reached for the box, her teary smile easing another worry from his heart. The ring inside came from the fly rod he'd broken during his first lesson. Her reaction told him he'd been right to save it for the occasion.

"We'll shop for a real diamond later," he assured, slipping the plain brass band onto her finger. "Until then…" He rose and swept her into his arms for a kiss that also promised more later. In the privacy of his bedroom.

When they'd kissed enough to seal the bargain, and with Jess settled in his arms, they called to Adam. The boy had reached the curving point at the end of the cove and was meandering his way back to them. The slower pace allowed just enough time for the last—and possibly the toughest—question Dan had to ask.

"Jess, I want us to be a family. I'd like to adopt Adam, if you'll let me. If it's okay with him. Would that be all right with you?"

In his arms, Jess tilted her head to stare up at him. Wonder and something else—doubt?—filled her eyes. "Adoption's a big step," she said, running a hand through her hair. "It's more than father-son picnics and fishing on Sunday afternoons. It's making sure he eats his vegetables, learns his multiplication tables. Staying up all night with him when he comes down with a stomach virus."

He caught her fingers in his own. "I'm good with all that. I'm in this for the long haul. Besides…" He kissed her fingers and grinned down at the face he looked forward to seeing the first thing every morning for the rest of his life. "I'm a doctor, Jess. I can handle the bedside thing."

"And you're sure this is what you want?"

"More than anything else." If it was up to him, he'd adopt Adam today and take away the slim chance the boy would ever have to face the past he'd had. But adoption took time and the courts moved slowly. "If we put things in motion now, we can finalize the paperwork as soon as we're married."

"About that…" Jess stepped out of his arms. She searched his face, slipped her hand into his and led them toward the shade, the table and chairs. "Have you thought about a date?"

"Not specifically." He ran a hand through his hair. "We'll plan on a big wedding, one with all the froufrou a girl wants at these things. I know that takes time." He frowned, not wanting to wait another day. "How about six months from now?"

A burst of laughter escaped her lips. He'd obviously gotten something wrong, but they'd run out of time to discuss it. Adam, who had finished his trek back from the edge of the cove, joined them at the picnic table.

"That was some big fish, wasn't it?" He spread his little boy arms as far apart as they would stretch. "I think it broke a world record. Do you think it did?"

"Maybe not quite, but it was a great fish." Jess bent to enfold her son in a tight squeeze. "And it's been a great day for me, too, because Dr. Hamilton and I have decided to get married. What do you think about that, kiddo?" She brushed her fingers beneath his chin, tipping his head up to meet hers while Dan held his breath.

His eyes widening, Adam swung to face Dan. "Does that mean you'll be my real dad?" he asked.

Dan took his cue from Jess. When her head bobbed

up and down, he said, "If you'd like me to, that's what I want."

Adam exhaled hugely. "Dad." He tried out the word while Dan fought tears. "Dad," he said again and pronounced it "cool," using his latest, favorite word. He turned to face Jess. "Can we eat now, 'cause I think I heard my stomach growl."

Laughter eased the rest of Dan's tension as Jess rose to her feet.

"Oh, you did, did you?" She brushed hair from Adam's face with one hand and wiped her own tears away with the other. "Now that you mention it, I could eat."

Later, after they'd put a fair-size dent in Maddy's chicken and brownies, Dan showed Adam how to work the digital camera. While the boy sipped sweet tea and they enjoyed the peaceful afternoon, he steered the conversation back to the wedding plans.

"What'd I get wrong?" he asked while Adam scrolled through the pictures of his catch for the hundredth time.

"Six months is nowhere near enough time to arrange for a church and a reception hall," Jess answered with the same odd look on her face he'd noticed earlier. "Let alone dresses and tuxes, caterers and florists and all the rest. Is that really what you want?"

He had to admit that it wasn't. He'd already considered all the people he'd invite to witness the day. Glen and Maddy would be there, of course. Sean and his sister. The other teens from Connections House. "I don't have a very long guest list."

"Good. Then, let's keep it simple." Jess reached for the water bottle she'd recently begun carrying and took a sip. Dan practically had to lean in to hear her quietly add, "And maybe sooner, rather than later. Because there aren't many gowns your bride will fit into six months from now."

"What?" It was Dan's turn to tease. "Now that you're going to be a doctor's wife, are you planning to eat bon bons and watch soap operas all day? 'Cause..." He stopped as the enormity of what she'd said struck home. Ice cubes rattled in a glass he could barely hold steady. He looked over the rim and read the truth in Jess's dark eyes.

"We're going to have a..."

She shushed him with a warning nod to the boy at the other end of the table, but the finger she placed to her mouth landed on a saucy grin.

Instinctively, he reached for her fingers and gave them a tight squeeze. "When?" he asked, awestruck.

Jess said, "About eight months from now, I think."

Dan let go of the breath he hadn't realized he'd been holding. "And here I thought life couldn't get any better," he whispered.

At the water's edge, a trio of sandhill cranes stepped carefully out from the brush. On impossibly thin legs, the birds stilt-walked through the sand before gathering their wings beneath them and taking flight. They soared, all grace and beauty, over the river as if they'd fly forever, but Dan had no doubt they'd be back. They'd made the preserve their home. Just as he'd found his home—and his future—in the heart of a feisty fly fisher.

He squeezed Jess's hand, secure in the knowledge that they'd made their catch and it was a keeper.

* * * * *

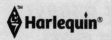
Harlequin®

COMING NEXT MONTH

Available July 12, 2011

#1361 THE TEXAN AND THE COWGIRL
American Romance's Men of the West
Victoria Chancellor

#1362 THE COWBOY'S BONUS BABY
Callahan Cowboys
Tina Leonard

#1363 HER COWBOY DADDY
Texas Legacies: The McCabes
Cathy Gillen Thacker

#1364 THE BULL RIDER'S SECRET
Rodeo Rebels
Marin Thomas

You can find more information on upcoming
Harlequin® titles, free excerpts and more at
www.HarlequinInsideRomance.com.

USA TODAY *bestselling author B.J. Daniels*
takes you on a trip to Whitehorse, Montana,
and the Chisholm Cattle Company.

RUSTLED

Available July 2011 from Harlequin Intrigue.

As the dust settled, Dawson got his first good look at the rustler. A pair of big Montana sky-blue eyes glared up at him from a face framed by blond curls.

A woman rustler?

"You have to let me go," she hollered as the roar of the stampeding cattle died off in the distance.

"So you can finish stealing my cattle? I don't think so." Dawson jerked the woman to her feet.

She reached for the gun strapped to her hip hidden under her long barn jacket.

He grabbed the weapon before she could, his eyes narrowing as he assessed her. "How many others are there?" he demanded, grabbing a fistful of her jacket. "I think you'd better start talking before I tear into you."

She tried to fight him off, but he was on to her tricks and pinned her to the ground. He was suddenly aware of the soft curves beneath the jean jacket she wore under her coat.

"You have to listen to me." She ground out the words from between her gritted teeth. "You have to let me go. If you don't they will come back for me and they will kill you. There are too many of them for you to fight off alone. You won't stand a chance and I don't want your blood on my hands."

"I'm touched by your concern for me. Especially after you just tried to pull a gun on me."

"I wasn't going to shoot you."

Dawson hauled her to her feet and walked her the rest of the way to his horse. Reaching into his saddlebag, he pulled out a length of rope.

"You can't tie me up."

He pulled her hands behind her back and began to tie her wrists together.

"If you let me go, I can keep them from coming back," she said. "You have my word." She let out an unladylike curse. "I'm just trying to save your sorry neck."

"And I'm just going after my cattle."

"Don't you mean your boss's cattle?"

"Those cattle are mine."

"*You're* a Chisholm?"

"Dawson Chisholm. And you are…?"

"Everyone calls me Jinx."

He chuckled. "I can see why."

Bronco busting, falling in love…it's all in a day's work.
Look for the rest of their story in

RUSTLED

Available July 2011 from Harlequin Intrigue
wherever books are sold.

ROMANTIC
SUSPENSE

Secrets and scandal ignite in a danger-filled,
passion-fuelled new miniseries.

**Family. Lies.
Full exposure.**

When scandal erupts, threatening California Senator
Hank Kelley's career and his life, there's only one place he can
turn—the family ranch in Maple Cove, Montana. But he'll need
the help of his estranged sons and their friends to pull the family
together despite attempts on his life and pressure from a sinister
secret society, and to prevent an unthinkable tragedy that would
shake the country to its core.

Collect all 6 heart-racing tales starting July 2011 with

Private Justice
by *USA TODAY* bestselling author
MARIE FERRARELLA

Special Ops Bodyguard by **BETH CORNELISON** (August 2011)
Cowboy Under Siege by **GAIL BARRETT** (September 2011)
Rancher Under Cover by **CARLA CASSIDY** (October 2011)
Missing Mother-To-Be by **ELLE KENNEDY** (November 2011)
Captain's Call of Duty by **CINDY DEES** (December 2011)

SPECIAL EDITION

Life, Love and Family

THE TEXANS ARE COMING!

Reader-favorite miniseries Montana Mavericks
is back in Special Edition with new loves,
adventures and more.

July 2011 features *USA TODAY* bestselling author
CHRISTINE RIMMER
with
RESISTING MR. TALL, DARK & TEXAN.

A Texas oil mogul arrives in Thunder Canyon on
business and soon falls for his personal assistant. Only
one problem—she's just resigned to open a bakery!
Can he convince her to stay on—as his bride?

Find out in July!

Look for a new
Montana Mavericks: The Texans Are Coming **title**
in each of these months

August	September	October
November	December	

Available wherever books are sold.

www.Harlequin.com

SEMM0711